His to Hold

TIA MARLEE

A NOVEL CHOICE

A NOVEL CHOICE PRESS

To my niece Lainey, whose love of horses rivals that of her momma. May you never lose your passion and your sass.

Contents

Chapter One

Caleb

The fluorescent lights in the back office buzz like they're personally offended I'm still here. I flip through the last of today's paperwork, signing off on vaccine records and updating a file for a dairy cow I treated at the Jacobson place this morning. Mastitis. Caught it early, thankfully.

Outside the window, Main Street is quiet. Most of the shops closed an hour ago; their windows dark except for the warm glow spilling out of Beats and Eats down the block. My stomach rumbles at the thought of their fried chicken, but I want to finish this stack before I call it a night.

The front door chimes, and I hear Austin's boots on the tile.

"You're still here?" He appears in the doorway, shrugging off his coat. Snow dusts his shoulders. "Thought you'd be halfway to the ranch by now."

"Wanted to get caught up." I tap the files into a neat stack. "Finn's got enough on his plate without me showing up late for dinner and making Patty hold everything up."

Austin grins. "How's married life treating him?"

"Good, I think. He smiles more. Patty's been good for him." I lean back in the chair and stretch, feeling the pull in my shoulders from a long day. "Of course, now Aunt Maggie's convinced the rest of us are next. She called my brother Cooper yesterday to ask if he was seeing anyone."

"And?"

"He hung up on her."

Austin laughs, a deep sound that fills the small office. He's a good guy, Austin. When I was looking for a place to set up practice after vet school, he reached out about partnering. Said Piney Brook needed a large animal vet, and he was tired of turning away farm calls. It's worked out well. He handles the dogs and cats and the occasional hamster emergency. I get the horses, cattle, goats, and anything else that lives in a barn.

"Speaking of calls." Austin pulls his phone from his pocket and glances at the screen. "Got one for you that just came in. After hours, but it sounds urgent. Horse down at a property out on Loris Road. Owner says the mare's been colicking for a few hours and it's getting worse."

I'm already on my feet. "Loris Road. That's only about twenty minutes from here."

"Eighteen if you hit the lights right." He hands me a slip of paper with an address and a name. Willow Dawson. "She sounded pretty scared on the phone. First-time horse owner, I think."

Colic in horses can go south fast. A few hours is already longer than I'd like. I grab my coat from the hook and check that my truck is stocked.

Emergency kit, IV supplies, sedatives, mineral oil. Everything I might need if this mare's gut has twisted.

"I'll call if I need backup," I tell Austin.

"I'll keep my phone on." He waves me off. "Go. And drive safe. Roads are getting slick."

The cold hits me the second I step outside. January in Arkansas isn't as brutal as some places, but tonight the wind cuts right through my jacket. I climb into my truck and crank the heat, pulling out of the small lot behind the clinic and heading east.

The drive gives me time to think. That's the thing about farm calls. Lots of time on the road. Usually, I don't mind it. Tonight my mind drifts to family.

Finn's settling in well at Apple Blossom Ranch. Uncle Harry and Aunt Maggie are down in Florida now, sending pictures of sunsets and fish tacos like they've been beach people their whole lives. Cooper called me last week asking about the ranch. If I had to bet, I'd say Coop will be back at the ranch before the year's up.

Colton's a different story. He's got his trail ride business going strong, and he's not ready to come back. I don't push. We all handle things differently.

The person I miss the most, though, is my baby sister, Holly. She's off in the big city for college, and we don't talk as much as I'd like. I make a mental note to send her a text after this house call.

The GPS dings, and I slow down, looking for the address. It's a small property set back from the road, a modest house with a barn behind it. The porch light's on, and I can see a figure bundled in a large jacket, standing in the open barn doorway, arms wrapped tight against the cold.

I pull up and cut the engine, grabbing my kit from the back seat.

A woman meets me halfway across the yard. She's younger than I expected, maybe late twenties, with dark hair pulled back in a messy ponytail and worry etched into every line of her face. Her boots are caked with mud, and there's hay stuck to her jacket.

"You're the vet?" Her voice comes out strained.

"Caleb Miller." I keep my tone steady, calm. In emergencies, people need an anchor. "Tell me what's going on."

"It's Clover. My mare." She turns and walks toward the barn, talking fast. "She was fine this morning, but when I got home from work, she was pawing at the ground and wouldn't eat. I thought maybe she'd work through it, but then she started trying to roll and I knew something was really wrong."

We step into the barn and the smell of hay and horse hits me. It's familiar, grounding. A single mare stands in the center aisle, her chestnut coat dark with sweat. She's shifting her weight, clearly uncomfortable, her head hanging low.

I set down my kit and approach slowly, letting her see me. "Hey there, girl. Let's take a look at you."

Willow hovers nearby, her hands twisting together. "Is she going to be okay?"

"Let me examine her first." I run my hands along the mare's side, feeling for bloating. Her gut sounds are quiet on the right side, almost absent. Not good, but not the worst I've encountered either. I check her gums. Pale pink, tacky. She's dehydrated.

"How long since she passed manure?" I ask, pulling out my stethoscope.

"I don't know. I didn't notice any in the stall when I got home, but I wasn't looking for it." Willow's voice cracks slightly. "I should have been paying closer attention."

"You called when you noticed something was wrong. That's what matters." I listen to Clover's gut, moving the stethoscope to different quadrants. The left side has some movement. The right is too quiet. "I'm going to sedate her lightly and do a rectal exam, see if I can figure out what's going on in there."

Willow nods, her face pale. "Okay. Whatever you need to do."

I work quickly and carefully, talking through each step as much for Willow's benefit as my own. The mare's cooperative, too tired and uncomfortable to put up much fuss. The exam reveals an impaction in the large colon. Serious, but treatable if we can get things moving.

"Good news," I say, stripping off my glove. "It's an impaction, not a twist. We've got options."

Willow's shoulders drop about three inches. "What do we do?"

"I'm going to tube her with mineral oil and fluids. It'll help soften things up and get her gut moving again." I move to my kit and start preparing the nasogastric tube. "She'll need to be monitored through the night, and I'll come back in the morning to check on her. This is treatable, Willow. She's got a good chance."

Her eyes are bright, and for a second I think she might cry. But she pulls in a breath and nods, steadying herself. "Okay. Tell me what to do. I can help."

"You can hold her head for me while I pass the tube. Keep her calm. Talk to her."

Willow moves into position, her hands gentle on Clover's halter. She murmurs something soft, and the mare's ears flick toward her voice.

5

"How long have you had her?" I ask as I work. Partly I want to know. Partly I want to keep Willow talking, keep her mind from spiraling into worst-case scenarios.

"Two years." She strokes Clover's neck. "I saved up for almost four years before that. She was the first thing I bought when I finally had enough."

There's a story there. I can hear it in the way her voice tightens around the edges. "She's a nice mare. I can tell you really love her."

"She's everything." The words come out simple, honest. "I know that probably sounds dramatic."

"Doesn't sound dramatic at all." I guide the tube carefully, watching for any sign of distress. Clover tolerates it well. "I grew up around horses. I know what they mean to people."

Willow glances at me. "You're one of the Millers from Barberville, right?"

I smile. "Yep. From Apple Blossom Ranch, actually. My uncle owned it for years. My brother, Finn, runs it now."

"I've driven past it. The one with all the apple trees?"

"That's the one. My great-great-grandfather planted those trees for his wife when they first bought the land." The tube's in place. I start the mineral oil, slow and steady. "Family legend says she was homesick, missed the orchard she grew up near. So he made her one."

Willow's expression softens. "That's really sweet."

"He was a romantic, apparently. Skipped a few generations, but it's in there somewhere." I don't know why I say it. Flirting in the middle of a colic case isn't exactly professional. But something about Willow makes me want to see her smile.

It works. Just barely, just a small curve at the corner of her mouth, but it counts.

"You from Piney Brook originally?" I ask.

She shakes her head. "Moved here about three years ago. I grew up a few hours north, near Mountain Peak."

"What brought you down here?"

"Needed a change." She says it lightly, but there's weight underneath. "I'd been saving for a horse, and land's cheaper here. Found this place, found Clover, and it just felt right."

"That's a big move to make on your own."

Her chin lifts slightly. "I like doing things on my own."

I file that away. Independent. Fiercely so. "Nothing wrong with that. Where do you work?"

"Piney Brook Elementary. I teach second grade." She smiles, a real one this time. "Twenty-two seven-year-olds, five days a week. They keep me humble."

I laugh, surprised by the warmth that spreads through my chest. "I bet they do. That's a tough job."

"It has its moments. But I love it." She looks down at Clover. "This is my peace, though. Coming home to her. Taking care of something that's mine."

The way she says it makes my hands still for just a second. *Something that's mine.* Like she's spent a long time not having things that belonged to her. Like this horse represents more than just an animal.

"She's lucky to have you," I say quietly.

Willow meets my eyes. In the dim light of the barn, they're a deep brown, almost black. "I'm the lucky one."

We stand there for a moment, the only sound Clover's breathing and the wind outside. A spark of something passes between us. I couldn't name it if I tried.

I clear my throat and check the flow rate on the fluids. "Almost done here. Then I'll walk you through what to watch for tonight."

"Okay." She nods, but she doesn't look away right away. Neither do I.

I finish administering the fluids and give Clover a mild pain reliever to keep her comfortable. Willow listens carefully as I explain the monitoring protocol: get her up and walk her every hour, no food, watch for pawing or attempts to roll, call me immediately if anything changes.

She asks good questions and types everything I say into her phone. She's scared, that much is obvious, but there's steel underneath it. She loves this horse, and she's not going to fall apart.

By the time I'm packing up my kit, Clover's resting easier, her eyes half-closed.

"She's a fighter," I say, giving the mare a pat on the neck. "And so are you."

Willow manages a small smile. It transforms her face, softening the worry lines and lighting up her dark eyes. Something shifts in my chest, unexpected and warm.

"Thank you," she says quietly. "I don't know what I would have done if you hadn't come."

"It's my job." Though somewhere in the past hour or so, this started feeling like something more than just a job. Willow intrigues me. I hand her my card. "My cell's on there. Call me if anything changes, even if it's three in the morning. I mean it."

She takes the card, her fingers brushing mine for just a second. "I will."

Outside, the temperature's dropped even further. My breath fogs in the air as I load my kit back into the truck. Through the barn door, I can see Willow spreading a blanket out onto a hay bale next to Clover's stall, settling in for a long night.

I climb into the truck but don't start the engine right away. Instead, I sit there for a moment, watching the warm light spill out of the barn and thinking about the way Willow looked at her horse. Like losing her wasn't an option she could survive.

Tomorrow morning, I'll be back to check on Clover. I find myself hoping the mare pulls through for reasons that have nothing to do with medicine and everything to do with the beautiful woman who loves her.

Chapter Two

Willow

The sound of Caleb's truck rumbling down the driveway leaves the barn quieter than before. I pull my jacket tighter and settle onto the hay bale I dragged over near Clover's stall. The cold seeps through my jeans almost immediately, but I don't care. I'm not leaving her.

She's mine.

The thought rises up fierce and sudden, surprising me with its intensity. But it's true. Clover is the first thing I've ever owned that really mattered. The first thing I saved for, worked toward, chose for myself. And I'm not going to lose her. Not like this.

Clover shifts in her stall, her hooves rustling the shavings. She's calmer now, thanks to whatever Caleb gave her, but I can still see the discomfort in the way she holds herself. I reach through the bars and rest my hand on her neck. Her coat is still damp with sweat, but her breathing has steadied.

"Clover girl," I murmur. "I really need you to pull through this."

She turns her head toward me and lets out a low whinny, almost like she understands. Like she's trying to comfort me instead of the other way around. My throat tightens.

I was ten years old when Dad left.

I don't think about it often. I've trained myself not to. But nights like this, when everything feels heavy, the memories creep in whether I want them or not.

He didn't say goodbye. That's the part that stuck with me the longest. One morning he was there, drinking coffee at the kitchen table and complaining about the news. By dinner, he was gone. Mom tried to explain it to me, but what can you really say to a kid?

Your father decided he didn't want this life anymore.

He didn't want *us* anymore.

She never said that last part out loud. She didn't have to.

After he left, everything changed. Mom picked up extra shifts at the hospital. We moved out of the house with the big backyard and into a cramped apartment closer to her work. And Maxie, my horse, the bay mare I'd loved since I was seven years old, had to be sold.

I understood. As much as a ten-year-old can understand, anyway. Horses cost money. Boarding costs money. We didn't have money anymore. It made sense.

But understanding something and accepting it are two different things.

I remember the day the new owners came to pick her up. I stood in the barn with my arms wrapped around her neck, crying so hard I couldn't breathe. Mom had to peel me away. She held me while we watched the trailer pull out of the driveway, and she cried too, which somehow made it worse. If Mom was crying, then it was really over.

I never saw Maxie again. Never saw Dad again, either.

First, my father left. Then my horse. And just like that, I learned that things don't stick. People don't stay. And when you love too much... well, *you're* the one left with a broken heart.

Clover nickers softly, pulling me back to the present. I blink hard and realize my cheeks are wet. I swipe at them with the back of my hand, annoyed with myself. This isn't helping anyone. Clover needs me focused, not falling apart over things that happened almost twenty years ago.

I pull out my phone and set alarms for every hour. Caleb said to walk her regularly, keep her moving. I'm not going to fall asleep and miss a single one. She deserves better than that.

As I'm setting the last alarm, I notice the business card still clutched in my other hand. I don't remember picking it up, but I must have grabbed it when I sat down. I smooth out the edges and study it in the dim light.

Caleb Miller, DVM. Large Animal Medicine.

His cell phone number is printed below, with a handwritten note in the corner. *Call anytime.* He underlined anytime twice.

A warmth spreads through my chest as I think about the way he handled Clover. Calm and steady, but gentle too. He talked to her as if she mattered, not like she was just another animal to treat. I sigh. He was so kind. Really, genuinely kind. Taking the time to explain everything to me and to make sure I understood what he was saying. It was after hours, and still he stayed. He didn't rush. Didn't make me feel like a burden.

I shake my head and tuck the card into my jacket pocket. I know where this road leads. I've watched enough friends go down it. They meet some guy and suddenly they're giddy, rearranging their whole lives around someone else's schedule, talking about the future like it's a guaranteed thing. And then, six months later, they're crying on my couch with a pint of ice cream, wondering what went wrong.

No thanks.

Men leave. That's what they do. Dad showed me that first. Every boyfriend I've had since then has proven it. They stick around until things get hard, until you really need them, and then they're gone.

I've built a good life here in Piney Brook. A life that belongs to *me*. I have my little house, my job at the elementary school, and Clover. That's enough. That's more than enough.

I don't need some handsome veterinarian with kind eyes and a gentle voice messing with my head.

Even if he does have a nice smile. And strong hands. And a way of looking at me like he actually sees me, not just through me.

I groan and drop my head back against the barn wall. "Stop it," I mutter to myself. "He's the vet. He's here for the horse. That's it."

Clover makes a sound that almost sounds like disagreement. I narrow my eyes at her. "Don't you start."

The first alarm goes off at ten. I haul myself up from the hay bale, my muscles already stiff from the cold, and let myself into Clover's stall. She's lying down, which makes my heart jump, but when I approach she lifts her head and looks at me with tired eyes.

"Come on, girl. Time to walk."

It takes some coaxing, but she gets to her feet. I clip a lead rope to her halter and walk her up and down the barn aisle, slow and steady. She

14

plods along beside me, her head low, but she's moving. That has to be a good sign.

"You're doing so well," I tell her. "Just keep fighting, okay? I need you to keep fighting."

We walk for about fifteen minutes before I put her back in her stall. She doesn't lie down again, just stands with her head in the corner, resting. I lean back onto my hay bale and pull up a game on my phone to keep myself awake.

The hours blur together after that. Alarm, walk, rest. Alarm, walk, rest. By three in the morning, my eyes are burning and my back aches from sitting on hay. But Clover's still standing. Still fighting.

Somewhere around four, I doze off despite my best efforts. I jerk awake to my five o'clock alarm, heart pounding, and scramble to check on her. She's in the same position she was an hour ago, calm and quiet. I sag against the stall door in relief.

"Sorry, Clover. I didn't mean to fall asleep."

She blinks at me slowly, and I swear there's forgiveness in her eyes.

The sky outside the barn door is turning shades of peach and purple when I hear the crunch of tires on gravel. For a second, my sleep-deprived brain doesn't register what it means. Then I remember. Caleb said he'd come back in the morning to check on her.

I stand up too fast and have to grab the stall door as the barn spins around me. I haven't slept much more than thirty minutes all night. I probably look like a disaster. My hair's falling out of its ponytail, there's hay stuck to my clothes, and I'm pretty sure I have mascara smudged under my eyes.

But when Caleb appears in the barn doorway, bag in hand, all I feel is relief so strong it nearly knocks me over.

"How's our patient?" he asks, his voice warm even at this early hour.

"She made it through the night," I say, and my voice cracks on the last word. "She's still here."

His expression shifts. Warmth and knowing in his eyes. He sets down his bag and crosses the space between us, stopping just close enough that I could reach out and touch him if I wanted to.

"You look like you've been up all night," he says gently.

"I have."

"You did good, Willow." He holds my gaze, steady and sure. "She's lucky to have you."

Warmth is spreading through me despite every wall I've tried to build. It's just exhaustion. And the emotional toll of nearly losing my horse. That's all. I take a step back, putting distance between us.

"Let's see how she's doing," Caleb says, nodding toward the stall. As he moves past me to examine Clover, I catch the faint scent of coffee and cedar, and my heart does a traitorous little flip.

This is fine. He's just the vet. He's here for the horse.

I can handle this.

Chapter Three

Caleb

Clover's gut sounds were better this morning. Not perfect, but improved. I told Willow I'd be back tomorrow to check on her again, and to get some rest. Poor woman had dark circles under her eyes, hay in her hair, and looked like she might collapse if she stopped moving.

She didn't collapse, though. She walked me to my truck and thanked me three times before I finally drove away.

Now I'm sitting at my desk at the clinic, staring at a file I've read twice without absorbing a single word.

"You planning to actually do any work today, or just stare at that folder?"

I look up to find Austin's leaning against the doorframe, coffee mug in hand, one eyebrow raised a cocky smirk on his face.

"I'm working."

"Uh-huh." He takes a sip of his coffee. "How'd the follow-up go this morning?"

"Good. Mare's improving. I tubed her again, got some more fluids in. Gut sounds are coming back on the right side." I flip the folder closed. "I'll check on her again tomorrow."

"Tomorrow? On a Sunday?" Austin's eyebrow climbs higher. "That's three visits in less than two days."

"Colic's serious. You know that."

"I do know that. I also know you don't usually schedule daily follow-ups for an impaction that's already resolving."

I don't have a good enough response to that, so I just shrug. "I want to make sure she's out of the woods."

Austin studies me for a long moment. Then a slow grin spreads across his face. "She's pretty, isn't she?"

"The horse?"

"The owner."

I grab a pen and pretend to make a note in the file. "I didn't notice."

"Right." Austin laughs and pushes off the doorframe. "Well, Mrs. Patterson's here with her cat. Apparently Whiskers has been 'acting strange.' I'm guessing hairball, but she's convinced its something exotic."

"Good luck with that."

"Thanks. I'll need it." He pauses at the door. "Hey, Caleb?"

"Yeah?"

"It's okay to be interested in someone, you know. You're allowed to have a life outside of this clinic."

He disappears before I can respond. Which is probably for the best, because I don't know what I'd say.

The truth is, I *am* interested. I noticed the way Willow's whole face changed when I told her Clover was going to be okay. She told me she stayed up all night, walking that horse every hour and refusing to leave her side. She was sweet as can be, even when she was frazzled and worried out of her mind. I also noticed the way she stepped back when I got too close, like she was protecting herself from something.

I noticed all of it. I can't stop thinking about it. About her.

My phone buzzes on the desk. I glance at the screen and smile when I see Cooper's name.

"Hey," I answer. "You're actually using a phone like a normal person."

"Don't get used to it." Cooper's voice is rough, like he just woke up. Knowing him, he probably did. "Finn said you're settling in okay."

"Yeah, the clinic's been busy. Good busy." I lean back in my chair. "How about you? Where are you these days?"

There's a pause. "New Mexico. For now."

"For now?"

Another pause, longer this time. "I've been thinking about coming back. To Barberville, I mean. Maybe helping Finn out at the ranch for a while."

I sit up straighter. Cooper hasn't talked about coming home in years. He got his farrier license straight out of high school and took off on what he called an "adventure." He's been traveling the Midwest ever since, working with different horses and show circuits, building a reputation. The fact that he's even considering coming home feels significant.

"Finn would love that," I say carefully. "You know he's been stretched thin since Uncle Harry retired."

"Yeah." Cooper sighs. "I just don't know if I'm ready to be tied down, you know? The ranch is a commitment. A big one."

"It is. But it's also family."

"Family." He says the word like he's testing it out, seeing how it feels in his mouth. "Maybe. I don't know. I'm still figuring things out."

"Take your time. The ranch isn't going anywhere. And neither are we."

"Thanks, Caleb." There's a warmth in his voice that wasn't there before. "Hey, I gotta run. But I'll call again soon. Maybe I'll even come visit."

"You better. Patty's been asking about you."

He laughs. "Tell her I said hi. And tell Finn to stop working so hard. He's making the rest of us look bad."

The line goes dead. I set the phone down and stare at it for a moment, thinking about Cooper. About all of us, really. The Miller siblings, scattered across the country, slowly finding our way back to each other. Finn took the first step when he came home to run the ranch. Now I'm here, building a practice. And Cooper, who's spent years on the road with his farrier tools and his wanderlust, is finally thinking about it too.

If Cooper comes home, that means Colton and Holly are the only holdouts. Colton's got his trail ride business going strong somewhere in Colorado, and he's made it clear he's not ready to come back. Holly's still finishing up her degree in interior design. As of now, she plans to stay in New York after graduation. As much as I want us all together, I don't push. We all have our own timeline.

The front door chimes, and I hear Austin greeting another patient. I should get back to work. I've got files to review, calls to return, inventory to check.

Instead, I pull up Willow's file on my computer.

Willow Dawson. Clover, chestnut mare, twelve years old. Emergency colic call, January 22nd. Impaction in the large colon. Treated with mineral oil, IV fluids, pain management. Follow-up scheduled for January 23rd.

I add a note for a second follow-up. Monitor gut sounds and hydration. Ensure full recovery.

It's medically justified. Impaction colic can relapse if you're not careful. I'm being thorough. Responsible.

I'm also lying to myself.

The truth is, I want to see her again. I want to see the relief on her face when I tell her Clover's improving. I want to hear her voice, watch her hands as she strokes her horse's neck, maybe catch another one of those small smiles she doesn't seem to give away easily.

I close the file and run a hand over my face. This isn't like me. I came to Piney Brook to build a practice, to be closer to family, to put down roots. Romance wasn't part of the plan. Not yet, anyway. Not until I was established and sure of my footing. Sure that I'd make it here, if I'm being honest.

But Willow Dawson, with her fierce independence and her guarded eyes, and her all-night vigil in a cold barn, has thrown a wrench into that plan.

I think about what Austin said. Maybe he's right. Maybe noticing isn't the problem.

The problem is, I'm pretty sure Willow doesn't want to be noticed. Not by me, not by anyone. I saw the way she stepped back this morning, putting distance between us even as she thanked me for helping. There's a wall there. I don't know what's behind it.

But I want to find out.

My phone buzzes again. This time it's a text from Finn.

Finn: Dinner at the house Sunday? Patty's making pot roast.

Caleb: I'll be there.

Living in the cottage on the ranch property has its perks. I've got my own space, separate from the main house where Finn and Patty live, but close enough for family dinners and easy conversation. Best of both worlds.

Willow Dawson is a different story. But I've never been one to back down from a challenge.

I grab my jacket and head out to check on the Jacobsons' dairy cows. Work first. Everything else can wait.

But as I drive out of town, past the turnoff to Loris Road, I find myself slowing down. Just for a second. Just long enough to glance toward Willow's property, even though I can't see it from here.

Tomorrow, I'll be back. Purely professionally, of course.

Chapter Four

Willow

C aleb's truck pulls into my driveway at the same time every
evening. Six-fifteen, give or take a few minutes depending on
traffic. Not that there's much traffic in Piney Brook, but still. He's
consistent.

It's been five days since Clover's emergency, and she's doing better.
Her appetite's back. She's passing manure normally. Yesterday she even
tried to nip at my jacket pocket, looking for treats. All good signs, ac-
cording to Caleb.

He doesn't have to keep coming. I know that. After the third visit, he
told me she was out of the woods. But he offered to stop by for a few
more days, just to make sure. And I said yes.

I tell myself it's for Clover. I want the peace of mind, and having a
professional check on her is the responsible thing to do.

I'm not even sure I believe myself anymore.

The truck door slams and I watch through the barn window as Caleb grabs his bag from the back seat. He's wearing the same brown jacket he always wears, the one that looks soft and worn at the elbows. His boots crunch on the gravel as he walks toward the barn, and even from here I can see the easy way he moves. Unhurried. Comfortable in his own skin.

"Hey," he says when he steps through the door. "How's she doing today?"

"Good. Really good, actually." I gesture toward Clover's stall. "She tried to steal my granola bar this morning."

Caleb grins. "That's a great sign. Means she's feeling like herself again."

He moves past me to examine her, and I step back to give him room. This has become our routine. He checks her vitals, listens to her gut, asks me questions about her behavior. I answer, watch his hands move over her coat, and try not to notice how gentle he is with her.

It's harder than it should be.

"Gut sounds are normal on both sides," he says, pulling the stethoscope from his ears. "Hydration looks good. I think we can officially call her recovered."

Relief washes through me, even though I already knew she was better. Hearing him say it makes it real. "Thank you. For everything. I don't know what I would have done if…" I trail off. I've thanked him a dozen times already.

Caleb straightens and meets my eyes. "You would have figured it out. You're tougher than you think."

The words land somewhere in my chest and take up residence there. I look away, not sure what to do with them.

"So," I say, busying myself with Clover's water bucket even though it's already full. "I guess this means you don't have to keep coming by."

There's a pause. When I glance back, Caleb's watching me with a hint of disappointment in his eyes.

"I guess not," he says slowly. "Unless you want me to."

My heart somersaults in my chest. I focus on the water bucket. "I'm sure you have other patients who need you more than we do."

"Probably." He doesn't move. "But I like coming here."

I don't know what to say to that. The silence stretches between us, filled with things neither of us is saying.

Caleb clears his throat. "Listen, I should probably head out. But if you ever need anything, you've got my number."

"I do." I finally look at him. "Thank you, Caleb. Really."

He nods, holds my gaze for a beat longer than necessary, then turns and walks out of the barn.

I stand there listening to his truck start up and pull away. Clover nickers and bumps her nose against my shoulder pulling my attention away from the sweet vet who's taken up residence in my thoughts.

I reach up to scratch behind her ears. "Don't look at me like that," I tell her. "He's just the vet."

She snorts, which feels like her way of saying 'yeah, right'.

The next few days are strange. I keep expecting to hear Caleb's truck in the driveway at six-fifteen, and when it doesn't come, I feel the absence more than I should. Which is ridiculous. He was only here for five days. Less than a week doesn't create a habit.

Except apparently, it does.

I throw myself into work. January is testing season at the elementary school, which means extra prep for me and stressed-out seven-year-olds who need more patience than usual. By the time I get home each evening, I'm exhausted. I feed Clover, brush her down, and fall into bed before nine most nights.

It's fine. This is my life. The life I built for myself, on my own terms. It's enough. It's what I wanted. Right?

On Saturday morning, I'm mucking out Clover's stall when my phone buzzes. I pull it from my pocket, expecting a text from my mom or maybe one of the other teachers.

It's from Caleb Miller, DVM.

My heart stutters.

Caleb: Hey, it's Caleb. Just wanted to check in on Clover. How's she doing?

I stare at the screen for longer than I should. It's a professional follow-up. That's all. Vets probably do this kind of thing all the time.

Willow: She's great. Back to her old self. Tried to eat my hair this morning.

His response comes quickly. Like he's been waiting for my response.

Caleb: Ha. Sounds about right. Glad to hear it.

I wait, but nothing else comes. I shove the phone back in my pocket and get back to work.

Ten minutes later, it buzzes again.

Caleb: Hey, this might be out of line, but there's a fundraiser coming up at the community center. A Valentine's Barn Dance. Proceeds go to the animal shelter. I have to go because apparently the new vet is expected to show his face at these things. Any chance you'd want to come with me?

I read the message three times.

He's asking me out. On a date. To a Valentine's Day event.

Every instinct I have screams at me to say no. To keep things professional. To protect myself from the inevitable disappointment that comes with letting someone in.

But there's another voice, smaller and quieter, that remembers the way he looked at me in the barn. The way he said *I like coming here.* He made me feel seen in a way I haven't felt, nor allowed myself to feel, in a long time.

My thumbs hover over the keyboard.

This is a bad idea. I know it's a bad idea. Getting involved with anyone is a bad idea, but especially someone like Caleb. Someone kind, steady and genuine. Someone I could actually fall for.

Someone who could actually hurt me when he leaves.

Because they always leave. That's the one thing I know for sure.

Clover sticks her head over the stall door and watches me with her big brown eyes. I swear she's judging me.

"Fine," I mutter. "But if this goes badly, I'm blaming you."

I type out a response before I can talk myself out of it.

Willow: Okay. I'll go with you.

His reply is almost instant.

Caleb: Yeah? Great. I'll pick you up at 6 on the 14th.

I press my phone against my forehead and groan. *What am I doing?*

But underneath the panic is something that feels dangerously like hope.

I shove it down and get back to work. I've got a stall to muck and a horse to feed and absolutely no business thinking about Caleb Miller's smile.

Too late.

Chapter Five

Caleb

B eats and Eats on a Saturday afternoon is exactly what I need after a long week. The lunch rush has cleared out, leaving just a handful of regulars nursing coffee. The low hum of country music from the jukebox in the corner greets me as I enter. I slide into a booth near the window and nod at Patty's friend Jolene when she comes over with a menu.

"Hey, Dr. Miller. The usual?"

"Please. And a black coffee."

She scribbles on her notepad and heads back to the kitchen. I pull out my phone to check messages, but my mind keeps drifting to the text exchange from this morning.

Willow said yes.

I've been turning that over in my head all day. She said yes to the dance, but there was hesitation in her response. I could feel it even through the screen. Like she was fighting herself the whole time.

The bell above the door chimes, and I glance up out of habit.

Willow walks in.

She's wearing jeans and a burgundy sweater and her dark hair is loose around her shoulders instead of pulled back like she wears it at the barn. She looks softer somehow. More relaxed. Until she spots me and freezes for half a second.

I raise a hand. "Hey."

She recovers quickly, crossing the restaurant to my booth. "Hey yourself. I didn't expect to see you here."

"Best burgers in town." I gesture to the empty seat across from me. "You waiting for someone, or would you like to join me?"

She hesitates. I can see the debate playing out behind her eyes. Then she slides into the booth.

"I was just going to grab some coffee," she says. "I've been lesson planning all morning. I needed to get out of the house."

"Lots to do in January?"

"I didn't get my planning finished over the holidays, so now I'm a bit behind. I like to plan the whole quarter at a time. It makes life easier." She smiles, and the tightness in my chest loosens.

I laugh. "Sounds like you need more than coffee."

Jolene reappears with my mug and raises an eyebrow at Willow. "What can I get you, hon?"

"Just a coffee with extra cream and sugar, please. And maybe a slice of that apple pie if you have any left."

"Coming right up."

"So," she says, her tone casual. "The Valentine's dance. What exactly am I getting myself into?"

"Nothing too scary. It's at the community center. There's food, music, and a silent auction. Last year, they auctioned off a weekend at some cabin up in the mountains. Went for a ridiculous amount."

"And you have to attend because you're the new vet."

"Apparently showing up at town events is part of the job description. Austin warned me when I signed on." I shrug. "Small towns."

"Small towns," she agrees. "I grew up in one. Smaller than this, even. Everyone knew everyone's business."

"Mountain Peak, right? You mentioned it."

She nods, and for a moment she's somewhere else. "We had a little farm outside of town. Nothing big. Some chickens, a garden. And horses."

"Horses?" I lean forward slightly. "You had horses growing up?"

"Just one. A bay mare named Maxie." Her voice softens the way it does when she talks about Clover. "She was mine. My dad bought her for me when I turned seven. The rest were boarders, but they were fun to walk on a lead rope."

There's a sadness in her voice now. "Sounds like a great gift," I say carefully.

"She was." Willow's fingers tighten around her still-empty hands. "I loved that horse more than anything. I thought I'd have her forever."

I wait. The silence stretches, filled with things she's not saying.

"What happened?" I ask quietly.

Her expression shutters. Just like that, the warmth drains out of her face and she's back behind her walls.

31

"We had to sell her." The words come out flat. Final. "Things changed. We couldn't afford to keep her anymore."

Jolene arrives with Willow's coffee and pie, breaking the moment. Willow thanks her with a smile that doesn't quite reach her eyes.

I want to push. I want to ask what changed, why they had to sell, what happened to the little girl who loved her horse more than anything. But I can see the tension in her shoulders, the way she's avoiding eye contact with me.

So I let it go.

"Well," I say, picking up my coffee. "Clover's lucky you found her. Sounds like you've been waiting a long time to have a horse again."

Willow looks at me. For a second, I think she might say something. Might let me in, just a little.

Then she picks up her fork and cuts into her pie. "Four years. I started saving right after I graduated college. I'm just lucky I had a full ride, otherwise, I'd be paying off school loans still. Even without loans, it took a while to save enough, but I got there."

"On your own."

"On my own." There's pride in her voice, but something else too. Something that sounds almost like defiance. Like she's daring the world to take this one from her, too.

The pieces start clicking into place. The fierce independence. The way she stepped back every time I got too close. The all-night vigil in the barn, like she'd physically fight off anything that tried to take Clover from her.

This isn't just about a horse. It's about loss.

I think about my own family. The way we scattered after high school, each of us running toward something or away from something else. But we always had the ranch to come back to. We always had each other.

"Hey." Willow's voice cuts through my thoughts. "You okay? You got quiet."

I blink and find her watching me, a small furrow between her brows.

"Yeah. Sorry. Just thinking."

"About?"

I could deflect. Make a joke, change the subject, keep things light. That's probably what I should do.

Instead, I tell her the truth.

"About how brave you are."

She stares at me. "What?"

"Starting over on your own. Building a life from scratch. Saving for years to buy something you love, even though you knew how much it would hurt if you lost it." I hold her gaze. "That takes guts, Willow."

Her cheeks flush pink. She looks down at her pie, then back up at me. "I'm not brave. I'm just stubborn."

"Maybe they're the same thing."

She doesn't have a response to that. We sit in silence for a moment, but it's different now. Warmer. Like something shifted between us without either of us meaning it to.

My phone buzzes. I glance at the screen. Austin, asking if I can cover an emergency call.

"I have to go," I say, already sliding out of the booth. "Duty calls."

"Go save some animals." Willow's smile is small but real. "I'll see you on the fourteenth."

"Looking forward to it."

I toss some bills on the table, enough to cover my meal and Willow's coffee and pie, and head for the door. But I pause at the threshold and look back.

She's watching me. When our eyes meet, she doesn't look away.

I should keep things professional. Protect myself from getting too invested in someone who might never let me in.

But as I step out into the cold winter air, I know it's already too late for that.

Chapter Six

Willow

"So let me get this straight." My coworker Becca leans against the doorframe of my classroom, arms crossed, a grin spreading across her face. "The hot new veterinarian asked you to the Valentine's dance, and you said yes?"

I glance up from the stack of spelling tests I'm grading. "He's not hot. He's been nothing but professional."

"Uh-huh." Becca walks over and perches on the edge of my desk. "Professional with nice arms and a great smile, from what I hear."

"Who told you that?"

"Jolene at Beats and Eats. She said you two were having coffee together on Saturday and looking very cozy."

I groan. "Small towns."

"Small towns," Becca agrees cheerfully. "So? Tell me everything. What are you going to wear? How did he ask you? Is this a date-date or a friend thing?"

"I don't know what it is." I set down my red pen and rub my temples. "He texted me. Said he had to go to the fundraiser and asked if I wanted to come with him."

"That's a date, Willow. That's definitely a date."

"Maybe he just didn't want to go alone."

Becca gives me a look. "Girl. You are in serious denial."

She's not wrong. I've been in denial for a week now, ever since I typed okay and hit send. Every time I think about the dance, my stomach does a little flip that's equal parts excitement and terror.

"I don't date," I remind her. "You know that."

"I know you say that." Becca's voice softens. "But maybe it's time to try something different. You've been here for three years, Willow. You've got a good job, a house, a horse. Maybe it's okay to want something more."

I stare at the stack of spelling tests. Twenty-two second graders who can mostly spell "friend" and "because" now. Small victories.

"What if it goes wrong?" The question comes out quieter than I intended.

Becca reaches over and squeezes my hand. "What if it goes right?"

I don't have an answer for that.

The next few days pass in a blur of lesson plans and cold weather and texts from Caleb that make me smile like I don't have a care in the world.

He sends me a picture of a baby goat he's treating at a farm outside of town. Its ears are too big for its head, and it's wearing a tiny sweater.

Caleb: Meet my new patient. His name is Frank.

I laugh out loud in the middle of the grocery store, earning a strange look from the woman in the produce section.

Willow: Frank is an excellent name for a goat.

Caleb: He has very strong opinions about everything. Reminds me of someone.

Willow: Are you comparing me to a goat?

Caleb: A very cute goat.

I'm still smiling when I get home. Clover greets me at the fence, tossing her head like she's been waiting all day to tell me something important.

"I know," I tell her as I let myself into the pasture. "I'm in trouble."

She nickers in agreement.

The thing is, I like him. I *really* like him. Not just because he's kind and good with animals and has a smile that makes my heart do stupid things. But because he sees me. The real me, not just the cheerful teacher or the independent horse owner. He saw me at my worst, exhausted and terrified in a cold barn at the crack of dawn, and he didn't flinch.

That scares me more than anything.

Friday night, I stand in front of my closet and stare at my options. The dance is tomorrow. I need to figure out what to wear, but every dress I own suddenly seems wrong.

Too casual. Too formal. I feel like Goldilocks trying to find the right bowl of porridge.

I pull out a deep green dress I bought two years ago for a wedding and never wore again. It's simple, fitted at the waist with a skirt that falls just below my knees. I hold it up to myself in the mirror.

"What do you think?" I ask the empty room.

The empty room doesn't answer. Which is probably for the best. That would require a whole different kind of house call.

I try on the dress. It still fits, hugging curves I forget I have when I'm wearing barn clothes and teacher polos every day. I turn sideways, then back. My reflection looks like a stranger. A woman who goes on dates. A woman who lets herself want things.

My phone buzzes on the dresser.

Caleb: Still on for tomorrow?

My heart skips. How could he know I am standing here panicking over our date? Outing? I don't know what I'm supposed to call it.

Willow: Still on.

Caleb: Good. I've been looking forward to it.

I read those words three times. *I've been looking forward to it.* Like this actually matters to him. Like *I* could actually matter to him.

The hope I've been trying to shove down rises up again, stubborn and insistent. I want this. I want to go to the dance with Caleb and laugh at his jokes and maybe let him hold my hand. I want to believe that not everyone leaves. That some people stay.

It's terrifying. But for the first time in a long time, the hope is louder than the fear.

I hang the green dress on the back of my door where I'll see it in the morning. Then I climb into bed and lie there in the dark, thinking about tomorrow.

About Caleb, and what it might feel like to let someone in.

Chapter Seven

Caleb

I change my shirt three times before I finally accept that I'm nervous.

This is ridiculous. I've given presentations to rooms full of veterinary professionals. I've handled emergency surgeries with steady hands. I've faced down a twelve-hundred-pound bull who didn't want his vaccinations.

But picking up Willow Dawson for a Valentine's dance has me standing in front of my closet like a teenager before prom.

I decide on a dark blue button-down and my good boots. Nice enough for the occasion, casual enough that I don't look like I'm trying too hard. I check my reflection one more time, run a hand through my hair, and grab my keys.

I stop at Blooming Joy's florist on Main Street in Piney Brook. The woman behind the counter smiles when I walk in, like she's been expecting me.

"Valentine's date?" she asks.

"That obvious?"

"Honey, every man in town has been through here today." She gestures toward the cooler. "What are you thinking? Red roses?"

I consider it for half a second. Red feels like too much. Too intense for a first date. "Pink," I say. "Do you have pink roses?"

Her smile widens. "Good choice."

She wraps a dozen soft pink roses in brown paper and ties them with a simple ribbon. They look right. Sweet without being overwhelming. Like something Willow might actually keep on her kitchen table instead of feeling awkward about.

The drive to Willow's place takes another fifteen minutes. I've made this drive a dozen times now, but tonight feels different. Tonight I'm not showing up as her vet. I'm showing up as her date.

Date. I asked her on a date. She said yes.

Don't mess this up, Miller.

I pull into her driveway and cut the engine. The porch light is on, casting a warm glow across the front steps. Before I can overthink it, I get out of the truck, flowers in hand, and walk to the door.

She opens it before I can knock.

My breath catches.

Willow's wearing a deep green dress that makes her dark eyes look almost black. Her hair is down, falling in soft waves past her shoulders. She's wearing a little makeup, just enough to notice, and there's a flush on her cheeks that might be nerves or might be the cold.

She's beautiful. She's always been beautiful, but tonight she's... radiant.

"Hi," she says, a little breathless. Then her eyes drop to the roses in my hand, and her expression shifts. Something soft and surprised. "You brought me flowers."

"Pink roses." I hold them out to her. "The florist said red was traditional, but that felt like a lot for a first date. Pink seemed more us."

She takes them carefully, bringing them to her nose and inhaling their soft scent. "They're beautiful, Caleb." She looks up at me, and there's a warmth in her eyes that wasn't there a moment ago. "No one's brought me flowers in a long time."

"Then you've been dating the wrong people."

She laughs, and the sound goes straight to my heart. "Let me put these in water. Come in for a second?"

I follow her inside and wait by the door while she finds a vase in the kitchen. Her house is small but cozy, full of warm colors and soft blankets, and pictures on the walls. It looks like her. Like a cozy little haven.

She sets the roses on the kitchen table, right in the center where she'll see them every time she walks by. Then she grabs a jacket from the hook by the door and turns to me.

"Ready?"

"Ready." I offer her my arm. "You look incredible, by the way. I forgot to say that."

The flush on her cheeks deepens. "Thanks. You clean up pretty well yourself."

She slips her hand through the crook of my elbow and lets me lead her to the truck.

The community center is already crowded when we arrive. There's a table set up for us to drop our coats. Strings of white lights crisscross the ceiling, and someone's decorated the walls with paper hearts and red streamers. A band is setting up on a small stage in the corner, and long tables line one side of the room, loaded with desserts and drinks.

"Wow," Willow says, looking around. "They really went all out."

"Valentine's Day is serious business in Piney Brook, I guess."

She laughs, and I instantly relax. I've been wound tight all day, worried about saying the wrong thing or pushing too hard. But standing here with her, watching her take in the decorations with that little smile on her face... I don't know what I was worried about.

We make our way through the crowd, stopping every few feet so I can introduce her to people I've met through the clinic. Mrs. Patterson. The Jacobsons from the dairy farm. Old Mr. Henley, who's had the same border collie for fifteen years and treats her better than most people treat their kids.

Willow handles it all with grace, shaking hands and making small talk like she's been doing this her whole life. I guess she has, in a way. Teaching second grade probably requires the same skills as navigating a small-town social event.

"Dr. Miller!" Austin appears at my elbow, grinning. "You actually showed up. And you brought a date."

"Austin, this is Willow. Willow, this is my business partner, Austin."

"The one who handles the hamster emergencies," Willow says, and Austin laughs.

"That's me. Nice to meet you, Willow. Caleb's told me a lot about you."

I shoot him a warning look. He ignores it completely.

"All good things," he adds, eyes twinkling. "Mostly about your horse, but I read between the lines."

"Okay, that's enough." I steer Willow away from Austin before he can embarrass me further. "Sorry about him. He has no filter."

"I like him." Willow's smiling. "He seems like a good friend."

"He is. Even when he's being annoying."

The band starts up, and a slow country song fills the room with fiddle and guitar. Couples drift toward the dance floor, swaying together under the string lights.

I turn to Willow. "Do you want to dance?"

She looks at the dance floor, then back at me. I can see the hesitation in her eyes, the same push and pull I've been watching since the day we met.

"Okay," she says finally. "But I should warn you, I'm not very good."

"Neither am I. We can be bad together."

That gets a real laugh out of her. I take her hand and lead her onto the floor.

Dancing with Willow is nothing like I expected. She's stiff at first, holding herself apart from me like she's not sure how close is too close. But as the song goes on, she starts to relax. Her hand rests more firmly in mine. Her body sways closer, until I can smell the soft floral scent of her shampoo.

"This isn't so bad," she murmurs.

"Told you."

She looks up at me, and something shifts in her expression. The walls she usually keeps so firmly in place are down, just for a moment. I can see the vulnerability underneath. The hope she's trying so hard not to feel.

"Caleb," she says quietly. "Why did you ask me to come tonight?"

I could give her a safe answer. *Because I needed a date. Because you're good company. Because it seemed like fun.*

Instead, I tell her the truth.

"Because I haven't stopped thinking about you since the night I showed up at your barn." I hold her gaze, steady and sure. "Because you're brave and stubborn and you love your horse more than anything, and I wanted to spend more time with you."

She stares at me. For a long moment, she doesn't say anything.

Then she steps closer, closing the distance between us until her head is resting against my shoulder. I wrap my arms around her and we sway together, not really dancing anymore, just holding on.

"I haven't stopped thinking about you either," she whispers.

My heart swells in my chest. I press my lips to the top of her head and breathe her in.

We stay like that for the rest of the song. And the next one. And the one after that.

Later, during the silent auction, I put in a bid on a couples' cooking class at a restaurant in Bentonville. It's a stupid impulse. We've been on one date. I have no idea if there will be a second one.

But when I win it Willow laughs and says, "I guess we're learning to cook together."

My heart soars. She's letting me in. At least a little bit. Whatever's happening between us, it's not just in my head.

I drive her home at the end of the night. The roads are quiet, the sky full of stars. Willow's hand rests on the center console, and halfway home, I reach over and take it.

She doesn't pull away.

At her door, I walk her up the porch steps and stop, not wanting the night to end.

"I had a really good time," she says.

"Me too."

She looks at me, and I see the question in her eyes. The same question that's been running through my head all night.

I lean in, slow enough to give her time to pull back. She doesn't.

The kiss is soft. Brief. Just a brush of lips, but it's the best kiss I've ever had.

When I pull back, she's smiling.

"Goodnight, Caleb."

"Goodnight, Willow."

I wait until she's inside before I head back to my truck. The whole drive home, I can't stop grinning.

For the first time since I moved to Piney Brook, the future feels wide open.

Chapter Eight

Willow

I wake up Sunday morning with a smile on my face and the memory of Caleb's kiss still warm on my lips.

For a few seconds, I just lie there, staring at the ceiling and replaying the night. The way he looked at me when I opened the door. The pink roses, soft and perfect, now sitting on my kitchen table where I'll see them every morning. Dancing under the string lights with his arms around me. The way he said he hasn't stopped thinking about me since the night he showed up in my barn. I giggle, wrapping my arms around myself.

And then the kiss. Short and sweet and somehow exactly right.

I press my fingers to my lips like a teenager with her first crush. This is ridiculous. I'm a grown woman. I've been kissed before.

But not like that.

And not by someone like Caleb.

I throw off the covers and pad into the kitchen to make coffee. The roses catch my eye immediately, their soft pink petals glowing in the morning light. I run my fingers over one of the blooms and feel a flutter in my chest again.

This is dangerous. I know it's dangerous. The more I let myself feel, the more it's going to hurt when it ends.

Because it always ends. That's the one thing I've learned.

But standing here in my quiet kitchen, looking at the flowers a man brought me because he wanted to see me smile, I can't quite make myself believe it. Not today. Today, I want to hold onto this feeling for just a little longer.

I take my coffee out to the barn. Clover greets me with her usual enthusiasm, tossing her head and nickering like she's been waiting all night to hear about my date.

"It was good," I tell her, scratching behind her ears. "Really good."

She bumps her nose against my shoulder, demanding more details.

"He brought me pink roses. And we danced. And he kissed me good-night." I laugh at myself. "I'm telling my horse about my love life. This is what my life has become."

Clover doesn't seem to judge. She just stands there, warm and solid, listening.

"I like him," I admit quietly. "I really like him. And that terrifies me."

She nickers softly, like she understands.

My phone buzzes during my lunch break on Wednesday. I'm sitting in the teacher's lounge, picking at a salad and half-listening to Becca complain about a parent who wants her kid moved to a different reading group.

Caleb: I can't wait to see you again. Are you free for dinner tonight? Nothing fancy. Maybe we can grab burgers at Beats and Eats around 6?

My heart does that little skip it's been doing every time his name appears on my screen. It's been three days since the Valentine's dance. Three days since he kissed me on my porch and drove away.

We've spent the time texting back and forth. Which has been a huge distraction. I find myself thinking about him when I should be focused on teaching fractions, or catching myself smiling at nothing.

"What's that face?" Becca leans over, trying to peek at my phone. "Is that the vet?"

I angle the screen away from her. "Maybe."

"It is! Look at you, all smiley." She grins. "What does he want?"

"Dinner tonight."

"And you're going to say yes, right?"

I look at the message again. Nothing fancy. Burgers at Beats and Eats. Like it's simple. Like we're just two people who want to spend time together.

Maybe it is that simple. Maybe I'm the one making it complicated.

Willow: Sounds perfect. See you at 6.

His reply comes almost instantly.

Caleb: Can't wait.

I spend the rest of the afternoon distracted. By the time the final bell rings and I've waved goodbye to twenty-two sugar-hyped seven-year-olds, I barely have time to get home, feed Clover, and change before I need to leave.

I stand in front of my closet, staring at my clothes like they hold the secret to the meaning of life. It's just burgers. I don't need to dress up. But I also don't want to look like I didn't try at all.

I decide on dark jeans and a soft cream sweater. Simple. Casual. Not like I spent twenty minutes agonizing over it. Now I just have to make sure I don't drop ketchup or burger grease on it.

Caleb's truck is already in the parking lot when I pull up to Beats and Eats. Through the window, I can see him in a booth near the back, scrolling through his phone. He looks up when I walk in, and he grins.

"Hey." He stands as I approach, and for a second I think he might hug me. Instead, he gestures to the booth. "I went ahead and grabbed us a table. Hope that's okay."

"It's perfect." I slide in across from him, suddenly nervous. This is different from the dance, where there were other people and music and distractions. Here, it's just us, a table, and conversation.

"How was your day?" he asks, settling back into his seat.

"Chaotic. We had an assembly this morning, which threw off the whole schedule. The kids were wound up for the rest of the day." I smile. "How about you? Any exciting animal emergencies?"

"Nothing too dramatic. Routine vaccinations, a dog who ate a sock, and Frank came in for a checkup."

"He's so cute in his little sweaters!" I grin, thinking of the last photo he sent me.

"His owner knits him a new one every week." Caleb shakes his head, but he's smiling. "She's convinced he gets cold."

"Does he?"

"Goats are pretty hardy. But Frank seems to enjoy the attention, so who am I to judge?"

I laugh, and the nervousness I was feeling fades away. Caleb is easy to talk to, and easy to be around. I don't know why I was nervous.

Jolene appears at our table with two glasses of water and a knowing smile. "Well, look who's back. Together again."

"Hi, Jolene." I feel my cheeks warm. "We're just having dinner."

"Uh-huh." She pulls out her notepad. "The usual for you both? Cheeseburger, extra pickles for the doctor. And let me guess, you're a bacon girl?"

I blink. "How did you know?"

"Honey, I've been doing this for thirty years. I can spot a bacon lover from across the room." She winks and heads back to the kitchen without waiting for confirmation.

Caleb laughs. "She's something else."

"She's intimidating"

"In the best way."

We slip into easy conversation while we wait for our food. He tells me about spending summers on the ranch with his brothers, the trouble they used to get into during apple picking season, and the way his uncle Harry would put them to work at dawn and they'd complain the whole time but secretly love it.

"You're close with your family," I say. I wish I was close with my family. After my dad left, Mom sort of checked out. Once I left for college, we hardly spoke at all outside of birthdays and holidays.

"Yeah." He nods. "We scattered for a while after high school. College, careers, all that. But we're finding our way back. Finn's running the ranch now. I'm here. Cooper's been talking about coming home, too."

51

"That's nice. Having people to come back to." I try to keep my voice light, but I'm sure I fail. It's a sore subject.

"What about you? Are you close with your family?"

I take a sip of water, buying time. "It's just me and my mom. We talk on the phone every few weeks."

"And your dad?"

I set my glass down carefully. "He left when I was ten. Haven't seen him since."

Caleb's quiet for a moment. "I'm sorry."

"It was a long time ago." I try to keep my voice light. "We got through it."

"Still." He holds my gaze, and there's no pity there, just understanding. "That kind of thing stays with you."

I don't know what to say to that. He's right, of course. It *has* stayed with me. It's the reason I'm sitting here with my walls half up, waiting for the other shoe to drop.

Jolene saves me by arriving with our burgers. They're massive, piled high with toppings, and I'm grateful for the distraction.

"This is incredible," I say around my first bite. "I don't know how I've lived here three years and never tried their burgers."

"Beats and Eats is a hidden gem. Don't tell anyone, or it'll get too crowded."

We eat in comfortable silence for a while. Outside the window, the sun is setting, painting the sky in shades of pink and orange. It reminds me of the night we met, the way the light looked spilling out of my barn while Caleb worked to save Clover.

"Can I ask you something?" Caleb sets down his burger and wipes his hands on a napkin.

"Sure."

"The other day, you mentioned your horse growing up. Maxie." He says the name like he's not sure he should. "What happened to her?"

My appetite disappears. I set down my own burger and stare at the table.

"After my dad left, things got hard. Mom was working double shifts just to keep us afloat. We couldn't afford Maxie anymore." I swallow.

"Willow." His voice is soft. "That must have been devastating."

"I was ten." I force a smile that doesn't reach my eyes. "I cried for weeks. But we didn't have a choice. That's what Mom kept saying. 'We don't have a choice.'"

"Is that why Clover means so much to you?"

I look up at him. His eyes are warm, patient. He's not pushing. He's just asking.

"I saved for years to buy her," I say quietly. "She's the first thing I've ever had that's really mine. Though, I'll be honest. Sometimes I worry that something will happen and I'll have to let her go."

"That won't happen, Willow. I'm sure of it."

"You don't know that." The words come out sharper than I intended. I take a breath. "Sorry. I didn't mean to be so harsh. I've just learned not to count on things lasting. People leave. Circumstances change. Nothing's permanent."

Caleb reaches across the table and takes my hand. His fingers are warm and steady around mine.

"I'm not going anywhere, Willow."

I want to believe him. I want it so badly it aches.

But my father said that too, once. Right before he walked out the door and never came back.

I don't say that. Instead, I squeeze his hand and change the subject. "Tell me more about Cooper. You said he might be moving back?"

Caleb watches me for a moment, like he knows I'm deflecting. But he lets me.

"Yeah. He's been on the road for years, working as a farrier on the show circuit. But I think he's getting tired of drifting." He smiles. "Finn could use the help at the ranch. And honestly, I'd like having him around."

"It must be nice. Having brothers who actually want to be near each other."

"Most of the time. We still drive each other crazy." He pauses. "What about you? Any siblings?"

"Only child." I shrug. "It was just me and Mom against the world."

"That sounds lonely."

"Sometimes." I look down at our intertwined hands. "I got used to being on my own. It's easier that way. Fewer people to disappoint you."

Caleb's thumb traces a slow circle on my palm. "It's also lonelier."

I don't have a response to that. Because he's right. It *is* lonelier. And sitting here with him, feeling the warmth of his hand in mine, I'm starting to realize just how lonely I've been.

After dinner, Caleb walks me to my car. The night air is cold, and I pull my jacket tighter around me.

"I had a really good time," he says, stopping beside my door.

"Me too."

He reaches out and tucks a strand of hair behind my ear. The gesture is so tender it makes my chest ache.

"Willow." He steps closer. "I meant what I said. I'm not going anywhere."

I look up at him, at his steady eyes and his gentle smile, and I want to believe him.

"Okay," I whisper. It's not quite trust. But it's a start.

He leans down and kisses me, soft and slow. When he pulls back, he whispers, "I mean it, Willow."

"Goodnight, Caleb."

"Goodnight." He waits until I'm in my car with the engine running before he heads to his truck.

I drive home with the taste of him on my lips and a war raging in my chest. Hope and fear, tangled together, so tightly woven, I can't tell where one ends and the other begins.

He said he's not going anywhere. Maybe he means it. Maybe this time will be different.

Or maybe I'm just setting myself up to get hurt again.

I pull into my driveway and sit there for a moment, staring at the dark outline of the barn. Clover's probably wondering where I am.

My phone buzzes.

Caleb: Home safe?

Willow: Just pulled in.

Caleb: Good. Sweet dreams.

I smile at the screen, then catch myself. He's breaking through my walls. This is exactly what I was afraid of. Letting someone in. Starting to need them.

But as I walk toward the house, the fear feels a little quieter than it did this morning. Maybe that's something.

Chapter Nine

Caleb

The smell of bacon hits me the second I walk into Finn and Patty's kitchen Saturday morning. Patty's standing at the stove flipping pancakes while Finn sits at the table with a cup of coffee, watching her like she hung the moon.

"Morning," I say, grabbing a mug from the cabinet. "Smelled breakfast from the cottage."

"That was the plan." Patty grins over her shoulder. "Finn said you've been holed up over there all week. Figured I'd lure you out with food."

"It worked." I pour myself some coffee and slide into the chair across from Finn. "How's the ranch?"

"Busy. Got a call from Cooper yesterday." Finn takes a sip from his steaming mug. "He's coming for a visit next month. Says he wants to talk about maybe sticking around longer."

"I was hoping he'd come to his senses and join us." I chuckle. "He called me a while back and hinted at it."

"Don't get too excited. You know Coop. He's not one to sit around in one spot for long." But Finn's smiling, and I can tell he's hoping, too.

Patty sets a plate of pancakes and bacon in front of each of us, then settles into the chair beside Finn with her own plate. He immediately reaches over and takes her hand, threading their fingers together like it's the most natural thing in the world.

A yearning takes up residence in my chest.

A year ago, Finn was happy to be single. Enjoying the ranching life in Montana. Then Uncle Harry decided to retire and leave the ranch to him on one condition. He had to get married. We all thought the ranch would be sold before that happened, but then Patty came along and changed everything.

Now they're married. Building a life together. Talking about the future like its something to look forward to instead of something to survive.

I want that.

The realization hits me like a horse kick to the chest. I want what they have. The easy intimacy, the partnership, the quiet moments over breakfast. I want someone to come home to. Someone who knows me inside and out and loves me, anyway.

I want that with Willow.

"You okay?" Finn's watching me with a curious look. "You've got a weird expression on your face."

"Fine." I shove a forkful of pancakes into my mouth. "Just thinking."

"About that girl?" Patty asks. "The one with the horse?"

I nearly choke. "How do you know about her?"

"Honey, it's a small town. News spreads fast." She grins. "Jolene said you two have been cozying up at Beats and Eats."

"We've had dinner. Once."

"And the Valentine's dance," Finn adds. "Austin told me you couldn't stop smiling for three days afterward."

I'm going to kill Austin.

"Her name is Willow," I say, giving up on pretending. "And yes, I like her. A lot."

Patty grins. "That's wonderful, Caleb. You deserve to be happy."

"It's complicated." I stare at my plate. "She's got walls. Big ones. I don't know if she's ready to let anyone in."

"The best ones always have walls," Finn says quietly. He glances at Patty, and something unspoken passes between them. "Doesn't mean they're not worth the effort."

Patty squeezes his hand. "He's right. Some people just need more time to trust. More proof that you're not going to go anywhere."

I think about Willow. The way she pulls back whenever we get too close. The way she deflects when conversations get too personal. She's been hurt. Badly. And she's spent her whole life building defenses to make sure it never happens again.

But I've seen behind those walls. I've seen the woman who stayed up all night with her sick horse. Who laughs at my terrible jokes. Who melts a little when I bring her flowers.

She's worth the effort.

She's worth everything.

"We have a cooking class tonight," I say. "In Bentonville. I won it at the silent auction."

"That's romantic." Patty beams. "What are you making?"

"No idea. That's kind of the point, I think."

Finn snorts. "You can barely boil water."

"Hence the class."

We finish breakfast with easy conversation about the ranch, about Cooper's potential return, and about Holly's latest adventures in New York. By the time I head back to the cottage to get ready, I'm feeling lighter than I have all week.

Tonight, I'm going to show Willow that I'm serious about her. That I'm not going anywhere, no matter how many walls she puts up.

I just hope she's ready to believe me.

The cooking class is at a little culinary school attached to a small restaurant and tucked away on a side street in Bentonville. It's intimate, maybe a dozen people total, all couples gathered around a large demonstration kitchen while a chef in a white coat explains what we're making.

"Italian night," he announces. "Fresh pasta, homemade marinara, and tiramisu for dessert."

Willow glances at me, a small smile playing at her lips. "Please tell me you know how to cook pasta."

"I can boil water. Does that count?"

"Barely," she says, chuckling softly.

She's wearing a soft blue sweater that brings out the warmth in her dark eyes, and her hair is down, falling past her shoulders in a cascade that has me wanting to run my fingers through it. She looks beautiful.

She always looks beautiful.

But something's different tonight. There's a tension in her shoulders that wasn't there before. A guardedness in her expression that makes my chest tight. She's not as friendly and warm as she was when I saw her last.

She's pulling away. Maintaining distance.

And I hate it.

The chef pairs us up at a station with all the ingredients laid out. Flour, eggs, tomatoes, garlic, herbs. Willow immediately starts sorting everything.

"You're very organized," I observe.

"Second grade teacher." She doesn't look up. "If I'm not organized, chaos ensues."

I step closer, close enough that our arms brush. She stiffens slightly, then forces herself to relax.

Something's wrong. My heart feels like it might literally break in two. Is it too late? Has she already decided to block me out entirely?

"Hey." I keep my voice low. "You okay?"

"Fine." She flashes me a smile that doesn't reach her eyes. "Just tired. Long week."

I don't believe her, but I let it go. For now.

The class starts, and we fall into the rhythm of cooking together. Or trying to, anyway. Turns out making fresh pasta is harder than it looks. The dough keeps sticking to my hands, and Willow has to rescue me twice when I nearly add salt instead of sugar to the tiramisu base.

"You really can't cook," she says, laughing. It's the first genuine moment we've had all night. I want to bottle the sound of her laughter and pull it out on rainy days.

"I warned you."

"I thought you were being modest."

"Nope. Genuinely hopeless." I hold up my flour-covered hands. "But I'm trying."

Her expression softens for just a moment. "You are. I'll give you that."

We work side by side, bumping elbows and trading quiet jokes while the chef guides us through each step. By the time our pasta is boiling and the marinara is simmering, we've found an easy rhythm together.

"This is nice," I say, stirring the sauce. "Cooking with you."

Willow doesn't answer right away. She's focused on the pasta, watching it like it might escape if she looks away.

"Willow?"

"It is nice," she says finally. But there's a hesitation in her voice.

I set down the spoon and turn to face her. "What's going on?"

"Nothing." She still won't look at me. "I'm fine."

"You've been quiet all night." I reach out and touch her arm. "Talk to me. Did I do something?"

She finally meets my eyes, and what I see there makes my heart clench. Fear. Uncertainty. The same look she had in the barn the night I told her Clover might not make it.

"I'm scared," she whispers.

"Of what?"

"This." She gestures between us. "You. How much I like you." She swallows hard. "I keep waiting for something to go wrong. For you to realize I'm not worth the trouble and walk away."

"Willow." I step closer, cupping her face in my hands. "I'm not going to walk away."

"You don't know that."

"Yes, I do." I hold her gaze, willing her to believe me. "I know because I've never felt like this about anyone. Every time I'm not with you, I'm thinking about you. When I imagine my future, you're in it."

Her breath catches. "Caleb—"

"I'm falling in love with you, Willow." The words come out steady and sure, even though I'm surprised they slipped past my lips. "I know that's probably too much too soon. I know you're scared. But I need you to know where I stand. I'm not going anywhere. Not now. Not ever."

She stares at me, eyes wide, lips parted. Behind us, the marinara starts to bubble. Someone at the next station laughs at something the chef said. The world keeps moving, but all I can see is her.

"I don't know how to do this," she says quietly. "I don't know how to trust that it won't fall apart."

"You don't have to know how. You just have to be willing to try." I brush my thumb across her cheek. "Can you do that?"

For a long moment, she doesn't answer, and I hold my breath waiting for the words that could change everything. I can see the war playing out behind her eyes. Fear, hope, hurt... her feelings on display one by one.

Then she nods. "Okay," she whispers. "I'll try."

I lean down and kiss her, right there in the middle of the cooking class with flour on my hands and marinara bubbling over on the stove. She melts into me, her hands gripping the front of my shirt, and for a few perfect seconds, everything else disappears.

When we break apart, her smile is small but genuine.

"Our sauce is burning," she says.

"Worth it."

She laughs, and the sound fills me with hope. I want to make her laugh every day for the rest of our lives, just to hear that sound.

We salvage the marinara and finish the class. The pasta's a little over-cooked, and the tiramisu is lopsided, but we made it together. That's what matters.

On the drive home, Willow reaches across the console and takes my hand. We ride in silence, and I think about Finn and Patty at the break-fast table this morning. The easy way they fit together. The life they're building.

I want that with Willow. And I think maybe she wants it too. It's okay that she's scared. I'll be confident enough for both of us until she's not afraid anymore.

Chapter Ten

Willow

C aleb calls me every night at eight unless he's on an emergency call.
It started the day after the cooking class. I was curled up on my couch grading papers when my phone rang. Not a text, an actual phone call. I stared at his name on the screen for two rings before answering.

"Hey," he said, his voice warm through the speaker. "Is this okay? I just wanted to hear your voice."

That was two weeks ago. Now it's become our routine. Eight o'clock, no matter what. Sometimes we talk for an hour about everything and nothing. Sometimes it's just fifteen minutes before one of us has to go. But he always calls. Every single night.

Tonight, I'm already in bed when the phone rings. I answer with a dopey grin I couldn't stop if I tried.

"Hey, you," I say, greeting him.

"Hey yourself." I can hear the smile in his voice. "How was your day?"

"Exhausting. I had a parent meeting this evening." I sink deeper into my pillows. "Mrs. Lopez is convinced her son is gifted because he can name all the dinosaurs. I didn't have the heart to tell her that's just called being seven."

Caleb laughs. "Did you eat dinner?"

"Define dinner."

"Willow."

"I had crackers and cheese. And an apple."

"That's not dinner."

"It's dinner-adjacent."

He sighs. "Tomorrow night, I'm bringing you real food. No arguments."

"I wasn't going to argue." I close my eyes, letting his voice wash over me. "Thank you. What about you? How was your day?"

"Good. Busy. Saw Frank again."

"Aww, how's my favorite well-dressed goat?"

"His owner knitted him a new sweater. This one is green with little white snowflakes."

"It's almost March."

"I mentioned that. She said Frank doesn't follow seasonal fashion rules."

I laugh, the sound bubbling up from somewhere deep in my chest. This is what I love about talking to Caleb. Everything feels lighter. Easier. Like the weight I've been carrying around for years doesn't press quite so hard when he's on the other end of the line.

"I miss you," he says quietly.

My heart does that flutter it's been doing more and more lately. "You saw me yesterday."

"That was twenty-four hours ago. Too long."

"You're ridiculous."

"Ridiculously into you, maybe."

I roll my eyes, but I'm smiling so hard my cheeks hurt. "Goodnight, Caleb."

"Goodnight, Willow. Sweet dreams."

I hang up and lie there in the dark, phone pressed against my chest. Two weeks ago, I told him I'd try. I didn't know what that meant, not really. I just knew I didn't want to lose him.

Now I'm starting to understand.

Trying means answering the phone every night at eight. It means letting myself laugh without waiting for the other shoe to drop and imagining a future that includes someone else and not immediately shutting that thought down.

I'm starting to believe that maybe, not everyone leaves.

The next evening, Caleb shows up at my door with a paper bag from Beats and Eats and a bouquet of wildflowers.

"Dinner," he announces, holding up the bag. "Real food. As promised."

I take the flowers and bury my nose in them. "You didn't have to do this."

"I wanted to." He steps inside, dropping a kiss on my forehead as he passes. "Where are your plates?"

We eat at my kitchen table, the pink roses from Valentine's Day long gone but replaced by the wildflowers now on display in the same vase. Caleb tells me about a complicated surgery he assisted Austin with today, some kind of tumor removal on a golden retriever. I tell him about the kid who announced during sharing time that his mom is having a baby and "Daddy says it's going to ruin everything."

"Kids are brutally honest," Caleb says, laughing.

"It's my favorite thing about them. No filter."

"Must be exhausting, though. Being 'on' all day."

"Sometimes." I push a fry around my plate. "But I love it. They're at this age where everything is still magical, you know? They believe in things. Tooth fairies and Santa and happy endings."

"You don't believe in happy endings?"

The question catches me off guard. I look up and find Caleb watching me, his expression open and curious. A week ago, I would have said no without hesitation. Now...

"I don't know," I admit. "I want to. I just... haven't had much evidence that they exist."

He reaches across the table and takes my hand. "Maybe you just haven't gotten to yours yet."

My throat tightens. "Maybe."

"I believe in them," he says simply. "I believe that people can find each other and build something that lasts. I've seen it. My parents. Finn and Patty. Uncle Harry and Aunt Maggie." He squeezes my fingers. "I believe it's possible for us, too."

I don't know what to say. The hope in his eyes is so bright it almost hurts to look at.

"Caleb..."

"You don't have to say anything." He smiles. "I just want you to know that I'm in this. Whatever this is, wherever it's going, I'm in."

I turn my hand over and lace my fingers through his. "I'm starting to believe you."

"Yeah?"

"Yeah." I take a breath. "It's scary. But I'm starting to believe you."

His smile could light up the whole county. "That's enough for me."

After dinner, we sit on my couch and watch a movie. Halfway through, I give up pretending to pay attention and curl into Caleb's side. His arm comes around me automatically, pulling me closer.

"This is nice," I murmur against his shoulder.

"It is."

"I could get used to this."

He presses a kiss to the top of my head. "Good. Because I'm not planning on going anywhere."

I close my eyes and let myself sink into the moment. His warmth. His steady heartbeat under my ear. The way he holds me like I'm something precious.

For the first time in as long as I can remember, I'm not worried about what happens next. I'm just... here. Present. Happy.

Maybe this is what it feels like to let someone in.

Saturday morning, Caleb picks me up for a trail ride. He's borrowed a horse from his family's ranch, and we spend the morning wandering through the woods behind my property. The trees are just starting to bud, hints of green pushing through the gray of winter.

"Spring's coming," Caleb says, pulling his horse alongside mine.

"Finally." I lift my face to the weak sunlight filtering through the branches. "I'm ready for warm weather."

"We should do this more often. When it's nicer out."

"I'd like that."

We ride in comfortable silence for a while. Clover's hooves crunch over the fallen leaves, and somewhere in the distance a bird is singing. It's peaceful. Perfect.

"Can I tell you something?" Caleb asks.

I glance over at him. "Of course."

"When I moved to Piney Brook, I thought I knew what I wanted. Build the practice, get settled, figure out the rest later." He's looking straight ahead, but I can see the emotion in his profile. "I didn't expect to meet someone. I definitely didn't expect to meet you."

"Is that a good thing or a bad thing?"

He turns to me, and the look in his eyes makes my breath catch. "It's the best thing. *You're* the best thing, Willow. I know we haven't been together that long, but I already can't imagine my life without you in it."

I pull Clover to a stop. Caleb does the same.

"I can't imagine my life without you either," I say quietly. "And that used to scare me. It still scares me, if I'm being honest. But mostly it just feels right."

He reaches across the space between our horses and takes my hand. "I love you, Willow."

He said it before at the cooking class. But hearing it now, in the quiet of the woods with spring breaking through all around us, it hits differently. Deeper.

"I love you too."

The words come out easier than I expected. Like they've been waiting there all along, just looking for permission to escape.

Caleb's face breaks into the most beautiful smile I've ever seen. He tugs on my hand, pulling me closer, and kisses me right there in the middle of the trail with our horses huffing impatiently beneath us.

When we break apart, I'm laughing. Actually laughing. The kind of laugh that comes from pure, uncomplicated joy.

"I love you," I say again, just because I can.

"I love you too." He's still grinning. "I'm going to want to hear that a lot, you know."

"I think I can manage that."

We ride back to the barn with our hands linked between the horses, and I think about what he said.

Happy endings.

Maybe I'm finally starting to believe in them after all.

Chapter Eleven

Caleb

I'm in love.

It's not a new realization. I told Willow weeks ago, and I meant it. But lately it's become nearly all I can think about. Every morning I wake up thinking about her. Every night I fall asleep with her voice still echoing in my head from our phone call.

I've dated before. I've even thought I was in love before. But this is different. Willow isn't just someone I enjoy spending time with. She's someone I want to build a life with. A family.

The thought doesn't scare me the way it probably should. It feels right. Like everything in my life has been leading me to her.

Saturday afternoon, I'm helping Finn repair a section of fence on the north pasture. It's tedious work, but I don't mind. There's something satisfying about working with my hands, about seeing the physical results of my labor. Plus, it gives me time to think.

"You're quiet today," Finn says, handing me another board. "Everything okay?"

"Better than okay." I position the board and drive a nail through it. "I've been thinking."

"About?"

"Willow."

Finn grins. "When are you *not* thinking about Willow?"

"Fair point." I grab another nail. "But this is different. I've been thinking about the future. Our future."

He pauses, setting down his hammer. "What kind of future are we talking about here?"

I take a breath. This is the first time I've said it out loud to anyone. "I want to marry her, Finn."

His eyebrows shoot up. "Already? You've only been together a couple months."

"I know. I'm not saying I'm going to propose tomorrow. But..." I look out over the pasture, at the horses grazing in the distance. "I know she's the one. I've never been more sure of anything in my life."

Finn's quiet for a moment. Then he nods slowly. "I get it. When you know, you know. That's how it was with Patty."

"Yeah?"

"Yeah." He picks up his hammer again. "I knew within a few weeks that I wanted to spend my life with her. Didn't matter that it seemed fast. Some things you just feel in your bones."

I do feel it. Deep in my bones, in my gut, and in my heart. Willow is it for me.

"There's something else," I say, driving another nail. "I've been thinking about where we'd live. If things keep going the way they're going."

"Her place is nice. Small, but nice," Finn says.

"It is. But I was thinking about something different." I set down the hammer and turn to face him. "What would you say if I wanted to build a house on the ranch property?"

Finn's eyes widen. "Here? On Apple Blossom?"

"There's that spot near the east pasture, where the land slopes down toward the creek. I've always loved that view." I can picture it perfectly. A house with a big porch, facing the pasture. Room for a barn. "Willow could have her horse right there. She could wake up every morning and look out the window and see them grazing."

Finn stares at me for a long moment. Then a slow smile spreads across his face. "You've really thought about this."

"I have."

"You're serious."

"Dead serious." I meet his eyes. "I know it's a lot to ask. This is your ranch now. If you'd rather I didn't—"

"Caleb." He cuts me off, clapping a hand on my shoulder. "This ranch belongs to our *family*. *All* of us. There's nothing I'd love more than having you build a life here." He squeezes my shoulder. "And if Cooper comes back like he's talking about, maybe he'll want to build something, too. We could turn this place into a real family compound."

The image dances through my mind. All of us, here. Raising families. Growing old together. Carrying on what our grandparents started.

"You really mean that?"

"Of course I do." Finn's smile is genuine. "Uncle Harry left this place to me, but it's not just mine. It belongs to all of us. That's what family means."

"Thanks, Finn." My voice comes out rougher than I intended. "That means a lot."

"Just promise me one thing."

"What?"

"When you do propose, let me know first. Patty will never forgive me if she doesn't get to help plan some kind of celebration."

I laugh, the emotional moment popping like a balloon. "Deal."

We get back to work, but my mind is elsewhere. I'm imagining the house. Two stories, maybe. A big kitchen because Willow deserves better than the cramped one she has now. A primary bedroom with windows facing east so the morning sun wakes us up. A spare room or two that could someday be a nursery.

Kids. I wonder how many Willow wants to have? We've spoken about it vaguely, but never in detail.

I want as many as she'll give me. I want to teach them to ride horses the way Uncle Harry taught us. I want to watch Willow with them, patient and loving the way she is with her second graders. I want Sunday dinners at Finn and Patty's, our kids running around the yard with their cousins.

I want all of it. Every single piece.

That evening, I drive over to Willow's place. She's in the barn when I arrive, brushing Clover's coat and talking softly to her.

"Hey, you." She smiles when she sees me, and my heart stutters the way it always does around her. It's an overwhelming rush of *this is it, this is everything*.

She is everything.

"Hey yourself." I lean against the stall door and watch her work. "Clover looks good."

"She's been great lately. Really healthy." Willow runs her hand down Clover's neck. "I was so scared when she got sick. I thought I was going to lose her."

"But you didn't. She pulled through."

"Because of you." She looks at me, her dark eyes soft. "You saved her, Caleb. You saved both of us, in a way."

I push off the door and move toward her, taking the brush from her hands and setting it aside. "I didn't save you. You were doing just fine on your own."

"I was surviving." She steps closer, tilting her face up to mine. "There's a difference."

I cup her face in my hands. "And now?"

"Now I'm living." She smiles, and it's the most beautiful thing I've ever seen. "Really living. For the first time in a long time."

I kiss her, slow and deep, pouring everything I feel into it. The love, the hope, the certainty. When we break apart, she's a little breathless.

"What was that for?"

"Just because." I rest my forehead against hers. "I love you, Willow."

"I love you, too."

We stand there in the quiet of the barn, holding each other while Clover watches with mild disinterest. And I think about the future I'm building in my head. The house by the pasture. The babies. The life we could have together.

Someday soon, I'll get down on one knee and ask her to be my wife. But for now, this is enough. Her in my arms. Her heart beating against mine. The promise of everything still to come.

Willow Dawson is meant to be my wife. I've never been more sure of anything in my life.

Chapter Twelve

Willow

My mother shows up on Tuesday evening without warning.

I'm grading papers at the kitchen table when I hear a car pull into the driveway. Clover's already been fed, and Caleb isn't coming over tonight because he had a late emergency call, so I'm not expecting anyone.

I peek through the curtains and my stomach drops.

Mom's rental car sits in my driveway, and she's climbing out of the driver's seat with a suitcase in one hand and her oversized purse in the other.

This can't be good.

I open the front door before she reaches the porch. "Mom? What are you doing here?"

"Hello to you too, sweetheart." She leans in and kisses my cheek, leaving behind the familiar scent of her perfume. Too strong, like always. "Can't a mother visit her daughter?"

"You've never visited me before. Not once since I left for college. And, you didn't call."

She waves a hand dismissively. "Well, I'm here now. Are you going to invite me in or leave me standing on the porch?"

I step aside and let her through. She sets the suitcase by the door and walks into the kitchen like she owns the place.

"This is cute," she says, looking around. "Small, but cute."

"Mom, what's going on?"

She sighs and sinks into one of my kitchen chairs. "Mark and I are done."

Mark. The latest boyfriend. I've lost count of how many there have been since Dad left. There was Steve, then Michael, then the one whose name I can't remember, then Gary, then Mark. Each one was supposed to be "the one." Each one ended the same way.

"I'm sorry," I say, because it's what you're supposed to say.

"Don't be. He was a jerk anyway." She drums her fingers on the table. "I should have seen it coming. They're all the same, you know. Charming at first, then they show their true colors."

I move to the counter and start making tea, just to have something to do with my hands. "What happened?"

"Oh, the usual." She waves her hand like she's swatting away a fly. "He said he needed space. Space! After two years together, he needs space." She laughs, but there's no humor in it. "You know what that means, right? There's someone else. There's always someone else."

I don't know if that's true, but I don't argue. I've learned not to argue with my mother about men.

"How long are you staying?"

"Just a few days. Maybe a week." She sighs heavily. "I needed to get away. Clear my head. Figure out what's next."

A week. My mother, in my house, for a week.

I love her. I do. She's my mom. But being around her has always felt like standing too close to a fire and hoping not to get burned. She reminds me of everything I've tried to move past. The instability. The fear. The constant proof that love doesn't last.

The kettle starts to whistle. I pour two cups and bring them to the table, sliding one across to her.

"Thank you, sweetheart." She wraps her hands around the mug. "This is nice. Us, having tea together. We should do this more often."

We've never done this. Not once. But I don't say that either. There are a lot of things we don't say, I'm realizing.

"So." She crosses her legs and looks around my kitchen. "What's new with you? Still teaching?"

"Yes. I love it."

"That's good. Stable job. Good benefits." She nods approvingly. "Smart choice. You were always the practical one."

I'm not sure if that's a compliment or not.

"And the horse? Still pouring all your money into that thing?"

"Her name is Clover. And yes."

Mom shakes her head. "I never understood the horse obsession. Even when you were little, you were so attached to that animal. What was her name? Marnie?"

"Maxie."

"Right. Maxie." She picks at a chip in my table. "You cried for months when we had to sell her."

"I remember." I remember everything about that day. The way Maxie's ears pricked forward when the trailer pulled up. The sound I made when they led her away. The empty stall that haunted me until we were forced to move and leave my childhood home behind, too.

"It was for the best, though. Taught you not to get too attached to things. People, animals, whatever. Nothing lasts forever."

The words land like hot stones in my chest. I stare at my tea, watching the steam curl upward.

"I never wanted to sell her, you know," Mom says quietly. "But after your father left, we didn't have a choice. He took everything. The savings, the security, all of it. Gone overnight."

I look up. She rarely talks about Dad. Not the specifics, anyway.

"I trusted him completely," she continues. "Fourteen years of marriage, and I never saw it coming. One day he was there, the next he was gone. No warning. No explanation. Just a note on the kitchen counter saying he needed to find himself." She laughs bitterly. "Find himself. Like he was lost somewhere inside our life together and needed to escape."

"Mom..."

"I'm not telling you this to upset you." She reaches across the table and pats my hand. "I just want you to understand. I was exactly where you are once. Young, hopeful, convinced that love would be enough. And then I learned the hard way that it's not."

I pull my hand back gently. "I'm seeing someone."

I don't know why I tell her. Maybe because Caleb feels like the one good thing in my life right now, and I want to protect that goodness by speaking it out loud. Or maybe I want to prove her wrong. To show her that my story doesn't have to end like hers.

Mom's eyebrows rise. "Oh? Who?"

"His name is Caleb. He's a veterinarian."

"A vet?" She sounds skeptical. "How long have you been together?"

"A few months."

"Hmm." She studies me. "And it's serious?"

"Yes." The word comes out stronger than I expected. "It's serious. I love him."

Mom's expression shifts. The joy leaves her eyes replaced by sadness and pity. "Oh, honey."

"What?"

"Nothing." She leans back in her chair. "Just be careful, okay? I know how this goes. Everything feels perfect at the beginning. He says all the right things, makes all the right promises. But men don't stay, Willow. That's the one thing I've learned. They all leave eventually."

"Caleb's not like that."

"That's what I said about your father. And Steve. And Michael. And Mark." She ticks them off on her fingers. "They're *all* like that, sweetheart. Some just take longer to show it than others."

"He's different," I insist, but my voice wavers. "He's kind. He's steady. He shows up every single day."

"So did your father. So did Mark. For two years, he showed up. And then one day, he didn't." She shrugs. "That's how it works. They're wonderful until they're not. They stay until they don't. And you're the one left picking up the pieces."

I want to argue. I want to tell her she's wrong, that Caleb is different, that what we have is real. But the words stick in my throat.

Because part of me has been waiting for proof that my fears are justified. Waiting for someone to confirm what I've always believed deep down.

Nothing lasts. Everyone leaves. It's only a matter of time.

"I'm just trying to protect you," Mom says, her voice softening. "I don't want you to end up like me. Fifty-two years old and starting over again for the hundredth time. It's exhausting, Willow. And it hurts. Every single time, it hurts."

I look at my mother. Really look at her. The lines around her eyes, the gray roots showing at her temples, the weariness that clings to her like a second skin. This is what a lifetime of loving and losing looks like.

Is this my future?

"I'm tired," I say, abandoning the tea. "I'm going to bed. There are sheets in the hall closet if you want to make up the couch."

"Willow—"

"Goodnight, Mom."

I escape to my bedroom and close the door behind me. My phone sits on the nightstand. Caleb's last text glows on the screen.

Caleb: Emergency call ran late. Missing you. Call tomorrow?

I should respond and tell him my mom showed up unexpectedly. I should let him be there for me the way he always is.

Instead, I turn off the phone and lie in the dark, staring at the ceiling.

Mom's words echo in my head. *They all leave eventually.*

I think about Caleb. His steady presence. His kind eyes. The way he talks about building a future together, like it's the most natural thing in the world.

What if she's right?

What if I'm just setting myself up for the same heartbreak she's experienced over and over? What if I let myself believe that a relationship with Caleb could work? Let myself depend on him, and then one day he wakes up and decides he doesn't want this life anymore?

The fear that's been quiet for weeks roars back to life, louder than ever.

I was stupid to think I could have this. Stupid to believe that my story could end differently than my mother's.

By the time I fall asleep, I've convinced myself I have to end things with Caleb. Before he has the chance to leave me first.

I have to protect my heart.

Chapter Thirteen

Caleb

Something's wrong.

Willow didn't respond to my text this morning, or my call this afternoon. Now it's almost five and I still haven't heard from her.

This isn't like her at all. We talk every day. Multiple times a day. Even when she's busy with school stuff, she always finds a minute to check in.

I try to focus on work, but my mind keeps drifting. Maybe her phone died, or she got caught up with something at school. Maybe something happened with Clover. Surely she'd call me, right?

Maybe I'm overreacting.

But the knot in my stomach says otherwise.

By six o'clock, I can't take it anymore. I tell Austin I'm heading out and drive straight to Willow's place.

Her car is in the driveway. So is another one that I don't recognize. A rental, by the looks of it.

I knock on the door and wait. It takes longer than usual for her to answer, and when she does, my heart sinks.

She looks tired. Not just physically tired, but worn down in a way I haven't seen since the night Clover got sick. Her eyes are red-rimmed, and she won't quite meet my gaze.

"Caleb." She says my name like it hurts. "I wasn't expecting you."

"You weren't answering your phone. I got worried." I search her face, trying to understand. "What's going on? Are you okay?"

She glances over her shoulder, then steps outside and closes the door behind her. "My mom's here. She showed up last night."

"Your mom?" I didn't even know her mom was planning to visit. "Is everything all right?"

"She and her boyfriend broke up. She needed somewhere to go." Willow wraps her arms around herself even though it's not that cold. "Caleb, we need to talk."

Four words. Four words that have never preceded anything good in the history of relationships.

"Okay," I say slowly. "Let's talk."

She walks toward the barn, and I follow. My heart is pounding harder with every step. Something is very, very wrong.

Inside the barn, Clover nickers a greeting. Willow doesn't acknowledge her. She just stands in the middle of the aisle, arms still wrapped around herself, staring at the ground.

"Willow. You're scaring me. What's happening?"

She takes a breath. When she looks up, there are tears in her eyes.

"I can't do this anymore."

I feel like I went three rounds with a heavyweight boxer. "Can't do what?"

"This. Us." She gestures between us. "I thought I could, but I can't. I'm not built for this, Caleb."

"What are you talking about?" I step toward her, but she steps back. The distance feels like a canyon. "Two days ago, everything was fine. Better than fine. You told me you loved me."

"I know." Her voice cracks. "And I meant it. That's the problem."

"How is that a problem?"

"Because it's going to end." The tears spill over now, tracking down her cheeks. "Maybe not today, maybe not next month or next year, but eventually. It always ends. And I can't go through that. I can't let myself love you this much and then lose you."

"Willow." I close the distance between us and take her hands. They're trembling. "You're not going to lose me. I'm right here. I'm not going anywhere."

"You don't know that." She pulls her hands away. "Everyone says that. My dad said that. My mom's boyfriends all said that. They all said the right things, and then they left anyway."

"I'm not them."

"How do I know that?" Her voice rises, raw and desperate. "How do I know you won't wake up one day and decide you don't want this anymore? That you don't want me?"

"Because I know who I am." I keep my voice steady even though everything inside me is falling apart. "I know what I want. And what I want is you. Today, tomorrow, for the rest of my life."

She shakes her head, backing away. "Don't say that."

"It's true."

"It doesn't matter if it's true right now. It won't be true forever. Nothing is true forever." She wipes her cheeks with the back of her hand. "I'm sorry, Caleb. I really am. But I have to protect myself. I have to end this before it destroys me."

I stare at her. This woman I love. This woman I was planning to propose to. This woman who's standing in front of me, terrified of a future that hasn't even happened yet.

"So that's it?" My voice comes out rougher than I intended. "You're just going to give up on us because you're scared?"

"I'm not giving up. I'm being realistic."

"No, you're letting your fear make decisions for you." The words come out harder than I mean them to, and I force myself to soften. "Willow, I love you. I want to build a life with you. But I can't do that alone. You have to want it, too."

"I do want it." The admission seems to surprise her as much as it surprises me. "That's what makes this so hard. I want it so much it frightens me."

"Then don't walk away. Stay. Fight for this. Fight for *us.*"

For a moment, I see it. A flicker of hope in her eyes. A crack in the wall she's building between us.

Then it's gone.

"I can't." She takes another step back. "I'm sorry. I know this isn't fair to you. But I can't be what you need. I'm too broken."

"You're not broken," I insist, pleading with her.

"I am." She's crying openly now, tears streaming down her face. "I've been broken since I was ten years old, and I don't know how to fix it. I thought maybe you could, but that's not fair either. It's not your job to fix me."

"I don't want to fix you. I just want to love you."

She closes her eyes like my words cause her physical pain. "Please don't make this harder than it already is."

I want to argue. I want to fight. I want to grab her and hold her and refuse to let go until she understands that I'm not like the others, that I would never leave her, that she's safe with me.

But I can see it in her face. She's already gone. Whatever her mother said to her, whatever fears came crawling back, they've won. At least for now.

"Okay." The word tastes like ash in my mouth. "If this is what you need, I'll respect it."

Her eyes fly open. "You will?"

"I'm not going to force you to be with me, Willow. That's not who I am." I hold her gaze, willing her to see the truth in my words. "But I want you to know something. I'm not giving up on you. I'm giving you space because you asked for it, but I'm not walking away. I'm not leaving. I'll be right here, waiting, for as long as it takes."

"Caleb..."

"I love you." I say it simply, like a fact. Because it is. "That doesn't stop just because you're scared. It doesn't stop just because you push me away. I love you, and I'll keep loving you, whether you want me to or not."

She doesn't respond. She just stands there, crying silently, looking more lost than I've ever seen her.

I want to hold her. I want to make this better. But she's asked for space, and I have to give it to her. Even if it kills me.

"Take care of yourself," I say quietly. "And if you change your mind, you know where to find me."

I turn and walk out of the barn. Every step feels like walking through wet concrete. Behind me, I hear Clover nicker again, confused by the tension she doesn't understand.

I make it to my truck before the weight of it crushes me. I sit behind the wheel, hands gripping it so hard my knuckles turn white, and try to remember how to breathe.

She ended it. Just like that. Days after telling me she loved me, she ended it.

I don't start the truck. I just sit there, staring at the barn, replaying every word of our conversation. Looking for the moment I could have said something different. Done something different.

But I know, deep down, that this isn't about what I said or did. This is about wounds that go deeper than I can reach. Wounds that have been there since she was a little girl watching her father walk away.

I can't fix that. She was right about that much. I can't fix what her father broke.

But I can show her that not everyone leaves. I can be patient. I can be steady. I can be here, day after day, until she believes it.

I think about the house I described to Finn. The big porch facing the pasture. The windows where Willow could watch her horses every morning. The nursery. The future.

It's not gone. I refuse to believe that. It's just... postponed.

I start the truck and pull out of her driveway. The drive back to the ranch feels endless. When I finally get home, I don't go to the cottage. I go to the fence on the north pasture and stand there, watching the sun sink toward the horizon.

Finn finds me there an hour later.

"Austin called. Said you left early." He leans against the fence beside me. "Everything okay?"

"Willow ended things."

Finn's quiet for a long moment. "What happened?"

"Her mom showed up. Said some things that got in her head." I shake my head. "She's scared, Finn. Scared that I'm going to leave her the way her dad left. So she decided to leave me first."

"That's..." He sighs. "That's rough."

"Yeah."

"What are you going to do?"

I watch the last sliver of sun disappear below the hills. The sky turns orange, then pink, then purple.

"Wait," I say finally. "Give her space. And pray that eventually she realizes I meant every word I said."

Finn claps a hand on my shoulder. "She will. Give her time."

"I hope you're right."

We stand there in silence as the stars come out, one by one. Somewhere across town, Willow is probably crying herself to sleep, convinced she did the right thing.

She didn't. But I can't force her to see that.

All I can do is be here when she's ready to try again.

Chapter Fourteen

Willow

The first morning without Caleb, I wake up and reach for my phone before I remember.

There won't be a good morning text. There won't be a call at eight o'clock tonight. There won't be any sweet messages, because I ended things.

I did the right thing. I have to believe that.

Friday, I go through the motions at school. I teach lessons, I grade papers, I smile at my students and pretend everything is normal. Becca asks me if I'm okay, and I tell her I'm just tired. She doesn't believe me, but she doesn't push.

The kids can tell something's different. Kids always can. Little Marcus asks me why I look sad, and I have to ask an administrator to come watch my class while I excuse myself to the bathroom for five minutes to pull myself together.

Mom is still at my house when I get home. She tries to be helpful, making tea and chattering about nothing, but every word feels like salt in a wound I'm pretending doesn't exist.

Saturday, I spend the whole day in the barn with Clover. I brush her until her coat gleams. I clean her stall twice. I reorganize the tack room even though it doesn't need it.

Anything to keep busy and avoid another conversation with my mom. Anything to keep from thinking about *him*.

It doesn't work. Every corner of this barn holds a memory. Caleb examining Clover that first night, calm and steady while I fell apart. Explaining what to watch for, his voice patient and kind. Kissing me in the middle of the aisle while Clover watched with mild disinterest.

I lean against her stall door and close my eyes. "I miss him, Clover."

She whinnies softly, like she misses him too.

Sunday morning, Mom decides it's time to leave, finally. "You're smarter than I was at your age," she says, hugging me at the front door. "You'll be fine."

I nod and wave as she drives away. Then I go inside, sit on my couch, and feel the emptiness descend around me like a fog.

I am not fine.

Sunday evening, someone knocks on my door. My heart leaps into my throat before I can stop it. I take a breath and try to squash down the part of me that hopes its Caleb. On unsteady feet, I head to the front door and look through the peephole.

It's not Caleb. It's Patty, holding a casserole dish. Disappointment floods me, and I'm fighting tears when I swing the door open.

"Hi." She smiles warmly. "I made too much dinner and thought you might like some. Finn's working late and we don't need all these leftovers."

I stare at her. "Did Caleb send you?"

Her smile doesn't waver. "Does it matter? Everyone needs to eat."

I want to say no. I want to close the door and go back to my miserable solitude. But Patty's already stepping inside, and honestly, I haven't had a real meal in days.

"It's chicken, broccoli, and rice," she says, setting the dish on my counter. "Nothing fancy, but it's warm and it'll keep you going."

"Thank you." My voice comes out smaller than I intended.

Patty turns to me, her expression gentle. "I'm not going to ask what happened. That's between you and Caleb. But I want you to know that you're not alone, okay? Whatever you're going through, you have people who care about you."

My eyes burn. I blink hard, refusing to cry in front of this woman I barely know.

"I don't deserve that," I whisper. "I hurt him."

Patty smiles softly. "I think you prefer to be alone right now." She reaches into her pocket and lays a card on the table. Caleb's handwriting is clear on the front. My name, written in his familiar scrawl. "I wrote my number on the back in case you need someone to talk to."

She leaves before I can respond. I stand in my kitchen, staring at the casserole dish and the card, and feel something crack inside my chest.

For a long moment, I don't move. I just stare at my name in his handwriting. Then, with trembling fingers, I pick up the card, remove it from the pink envelope, and open it.

Willow,

I know you're scared. I know you think you're protecting yourself. But I need you to know that loving you isn't something I can turn off. It isn't something I <u>want</u> to turn off.

You're not too broken. You're not too much. You're exactly who I want.

I'll wait as long as it takes.

Love, Caleb

The tears come before I can stop them. I sink into a kitchen chair, pressing the card against my chest, and I cry until I can't breathe. I cry for the little girl who lost her father and her horse in the same year. I cry for the woman who's spent her whole life building walls to keep out the pain. I cry for the man who loves me anyway, who refuses to give up, who's out there somewhere waiting for me to believe him.

When the tears finally stop, I'm exhausted. Hollowed out. But somewhere beneath the emptiness, there's hope.

I read the card again. And again. And one more time before I finally set it down.

Then I eat the casserole, standing at the counter, because Caleb wanted me to. I need to take care of myself.

Monday morning, I find flowers on my porch.

Pink roses. A dozen of them, wrapped in brown paper and tied with a simple ribbon. No card, no note. Just the flowers, sitting there like they've been waiting on me.

I know who they're from. I know what they mean.

I bring them inside and put them in the vase on my kitchen table. The same vase that held the Valentine's roses and the wildflowers he brought me.

I should throw them away. Keeping them just makes this harder.

I don't throw them away.

Tuesday morning, there's a small potted plant on my porch. A succulent, the kind that's almost impossible to kill. A tiny tag is tucked into the soil.

Still here. Written in Caleb's handwriting.

I carry it inside and set it on my windowsill. I stare at the two words on that tag until they blur.

Still here.

He's not giving up. Even though I pushed him away. Even though I told him I couldn't do this. He's still here, showing me in a hundred small ways that he meant what he said.

I don't know what to do with that.

Wednesday, Becca corners me in the teacher's lounge.

"Okay." She crosses her arms. "Spill. What happened with the vet?"

"Nothing."

"Willow. You've been walking around like a zombie for a week. Something happened."

I stare at my untouched salad. "I ended it."

"You what?" Her voice rises. "Why? I thought things were going great. You told me you loved him."

"I do love him. That's the problem."

"That doesn't make any sense."

"It does if you're me." I push the salad away. "My mom came to visit. She and her boyfriend broke up. Again. And she reminded me of what happens when you let yourself love someone. They leave. They always leave. And I couldn't..."

"So you left first." Becca's voice softens. "Oh, Willow."

"It was the smart thing to do."

"Was it? Because you look miserable."

"I'll get over it."

"Will you?" She leans forward. "Look, I don't know Caleb that well. But I know what you looked like when you were with him. You were happy. Actually happy, for the first time since I've known you. And now?"

"I'm protecting myself."

"From what? From being happy?" She shakes her head. "Honey, that's not protection. That's just a different kind of prison."

Her words hit too close to home. I stand up abruptly. "I have to get back to my classroom."

"Willow—"

"I'll see you later, Becca."

I spend the rest of the day replaying her words. *A different kind of prison.* Is that what I've built for myself? Walls so high that nothing can hurt me, but nothing can reach me either?

Thursday, I come home to find a bag from Beats and Eats hanging on my door handle. Inside is a cheeseburger, still warm, and a note in handwriting I don't recognize.

The doc said to give you extra bacon. Enjoy. - Jolene

I laugh even though I want to cry.

He got Jolene involved.

Of course he did.

I eat the burger standing at my kitchen counter, looking at the roses and the little succulent and the clean casserole dish I still haven't returned to Patty. Evidence of a man who refuses to disappear, even when I've asked him to.

My phone sits on the counter. I could call him. I could tell him to stop. I could tell him that every small gesture is making this harder, not easier. That I don't love him like I said.

But that would be a lie.

The truth is, every flower, every meal, every tiny sign that he's still there chips away at the wall I've built. The wall that felt so necessary a week ago is starting to feel less like protection and more like a cage.

I pick up my phone. Set it down. Pick it up again.

I'm not ready. Not yet.

But for the first time since I ended things, I'm starting to wonder if maybe I was wrong.

Friday morning, I wake up before dawn. I can't sleep. Haven't been able to sleep properly in over a week. Not since my mom showed up with her emotional baggage.

I pull on boots and a jacket and walk out to the barn. Clover's awake, watching for me like she always does.

"Hey, girl." I let myself into her stall and wrap my arms around her neck. She stands patiently, letting me hold on.

"I don't know what to do," I whisper into her mane. "I thought I was protecting myself, but I just feel empty. I thought the fear would go away if I ended it, but it didn't. It just turned into a different kind of fear."

She nickers softly in agreement.

"I miss him so much it hurts to breathe. And he keeps showing up in all these little ways. Like he's trying to prove that he's not going anywhere."

I pull back and look at her. Her big brown eyes are calm, steady. Non-judgmental.

"What if he's telling the truth?" I ask her. "What if he really *is* different? What if I threw away the best thing that ever happened to me because I was too scared to believe it could last?"

Clover doesn't answer. She just bumps her muzzle against my shoulder, the way she always does when she wants attention.

I stand there in the quiet barn, the first gray light of dawn creeping through the windows, and I feel something shift inside me.

I've spent my whole life running from the possibility of being hurt. Building walls. Keeping people at arm's length. Convincing myself that being alone was safer than being left.

But I'm not safe. I'm just lonely. And the man I love is out there, leaving flowers on my porch and sending casseroles and cheeseburgers and refusing to give up on me, even though I've given him every reason to.

Maybe it's time to stop running.

Maybe it's time to be brave.

Chapter Fifteen

Caleb

Waiting is the hardest thing I've ever done.

Every morning, I wake up reaching for my phone, hoping for a text that isn't there. Every night, I stare at the ceiling and wonder if she's okay. If she's eating. If she's sleeping. If she's thinking about me half as much as I'm thinking about her.

I throw myself into my work. It's the only thing that helps. When I'm elbow-deep in a calving or stitching up a lamb that tangled with a barbed wire fence, I don't have time to think about the hole in my chest where Willow used to fit.

"You look terrible," Austin says on Monday afternoon, catching me between appointments. "When's the last time you slept?"

"I sleep."

"Uh-huh." He crosses his arms and leans against the doorframe of my office. "And when's the last time you ate something that wasn't coffee?"

I don't answer. I honestly can't remember.

"Caleb." His voice softens. "What happened?"

"She ended it." The words still feel like glass in my throat. "Said she couldn't do it anymore. That she was too scared."

Austin's quiet for a moment. "I'm sorry, man. I know how much she meant to you."

"Means." I look up at him. "She still *means* everything to me. That hasn't changed."

"So what are you going to do?"

"Wait." I turn back to my computer, pretending to look at the appointment schedule. "Give her space. Show her I'm not going anywhere."

"And if she doesn't come back?"

The question hangs in the air. I've asked myself the same thing a hundred times since she ended things. What if she never changes her mind? What if I wait forever and she never believes me?

"Then at least she'll know someone loved her enough to try," I replied.

Austin doesn't say anything else. He just claps me on the shoulder and leaves me to my misery.

Ever since the break up, I've been trying to show her I'm still here. I couldn't just sit there and do nothing, so I asked Patty if she'd be willing to take a casserole and a card I'd written to Willow. I'd been hoping to hear from Willow after Patty got back home, but the phone never rang. That was Sunday.

Monday morning on my way to work, I saw the light on in Blooming Joy's, and begged for Joy to let me in.

"Goodness," Joy said when she finally opened the door for me. "We're determined this morning, aren't we?"

"Please tell me you have a dozen pink roses," I asked.

Joy looked me up and down before patting my arm. "Love isn't always easy," she said, heading to the back. When she came out, she was carrying the roses wrapped in brown paper. "Good Luck," she said as I left the store just as the sun was coming up.

I drove straight to Willow's place and left them on her porch for her to find when she left for work.

I didn't knock. I didn't leave a note. I just wanted her to know I was thinking of her.

That afternoon, when I went into the hardware store to buy some rope for my truck, I found a succulent and it made me think of Willow. Strong and beautiful, the kind of plant that survives on neglect. I tucked a tag into the soil with two words: *Still here.*

I left it on her porch before the sun came up on Tuesday morning, same as the flowers.

Then, on Wednesday when I grabbed lunch from Beats and Eats, I asked Jolene if she'd drop off dinner to Willow on Thursday. "A cheeseburger with extra bacon," I told her. "She loves those."

Jolene gave me a long look but didn't ask questions. "Consider it done, Doc."

Everyone keeps telling me to give her time. But time feels like the enemy right now. Every day that passes is another day she spends convincing herself she made the right choice. Another day her wall gets higher.

Now it's Thursday afternoon and I'm at the clinic trying to catch up on paperwork when the bell over the front door chimes. I look up, expecting a client, and find Ms. Daisy standing in the lobby with a paper bag in her hands.

"Ms. Daisy?" I stand up, confused. "Is everything okay? Is something wrong with one of your cats?"

"My cats are fine." She marches past the front desk and into my office like she owns the place. "You, on the other hand, are not fine."

"I'm—"

"Don't you dare say you're fine, Caleb Miller." She sets the bag on my desk and puts her hands on her hips. "You haven't been in for dinner all week. And I have eyes. You look like something the barn cat dragged in."

I don't know whether to laugh or cry. "I appreciate the concern, but—"

"No buts." She points at the bag. "That's a cheeseburger, extra pickles, just the way you like it. And you're going to eat every bite."

"Ms. Daisy—"

"I've known you since you were a boy running around this town with your brothers, getting into trouble and breaking hearts." Her voice softens, and she lowers herself into the chair across from my desk. "I know heartache when I see it, honey. And I know you well enough to know you're so busy taking care of everyone else that you're forgetting to take care of yourself."

My throat tightens. "How did you know?"

"Small town. Word travels." She tilts her head, studying me. "Jolene said you asked her to drop off dinner to someone tonight. A young woman on Loris Road. And Patty's been worried about you all week."

I should have known I couldn't keep anything secret in Piney Brook.

"I'm not giving up on her," I say quietly. "I can't."

"I wouldn't expect you to. You Millers are stubborn as mules." She smiles. "But you can't pour from an empty cup, sweetheart. You've got to take care of yourself too. Otherwise, when she does come around, you'll be too worn out to enjoy it."

When. Not *if*. I hold onto that word like a lifeline.

"Yes, ma'am." I pull the bag toward me and open it. The smell of the burger makes my stomach growl loud enough for her to hear.

Ms. Daisy laughs. "That's what I thought. Now eat. And I expect to see you in the restaurant this weekend. You've got the whole town worried sick."

"Yes, ma'am," I say again, and this time I mean it.

She pats my hand and leaves. I eat the burger slowly, tasting it for the first time in days. It's good. Really good. And somewhere between the first bite and the last, I feel the sadness in my chest loosen just a little.

I'm not okay. I won't be okay until Willow's back in my arms. But Ms. Daisy's right. I have to keep going. I have to take care of myself so I can be ready when she's ready.

If she's ever ready.

That night, Finn finds me sitting on the porch of my cottage, staring at nothing.

"Thought I'd find you out here." He settles into the chair beside me. "How you holding up?"

"I've been better."

"Yeah." He's quiet for a moment. "Patty says Willow looked rough when she delivered the casserole the other day."

"She's hurting." I rub a hand over my face. "She's hurting and I can't do anything about it. I just have to sit here and wait and hope she figures out that I'm not going to disappear."

"That's hard."

"It's the hardest thing I've ever done." I look at him. "How did you do it? With Patty? When things were uncertain?"

Finn considers the question. "I just kept showing up. Even when it felt hopeless. Even when I wasn't sure she'd ever trust me. I figured the worst that could happen was that I'd prove I meant what I said, and she'd still walk away. But at least she'd know."

"And the best that could happen?"

"The best?" He smiles. "The best is what I have now. A wife I love. A life I never imagined. A future I can't wait to build." He turns to me. "Willow's scared, Caleb. But scared doesn't mean done. It just means she needs more proof."

"I'm trying to give her that."

"I know you are." He claps me on the shoulder. "And she'll see it. Eventually. The question is whether you can hold on long enough for her to believe it."

I think about the roses that are probably wilting on her kitchen table. The succulent I left on her porch. The card with my heart spelled out in ink. All the small ways I've tried to show her that I'm not going anywhere.

"I can hold on," I say. "As long as it takes. Even if it's the hardest thing I've ever done."

Finn nods. "That's what I thought."

We sit in silence for a while as the stars dot the sky one by one. Then Finn stands and pats my shoulder before making his way back to his house.

I stare at the stars, imagining Willow looking at the same ones. "I'm still here," I whisper into the night. "Please choose us."

Chapter Sixteen

Willow

F riday morning, I wake up before dawn with a strange feeling in my chest.

It takes me a moment to recognize it. It's not dread. It's not the heavy weight of sadness I've been carrying all week. It feels almost like... hope.

I lie in bed staring at the ceiling, replaying everything that's happened over the last few days. The roses on my kitchen table. The succulent on my windowsill. The card sitting on my nightstand that I've read so many times I have memorized the words.

You're not too broken. You're not too much. You're exactly who I want.

I'll wait as long as it takes.

Becca's voice echoes in my head. *That's not protection. That's just a different kind of prison.*

She was right. I've been so busy protecting myself from the possibility of being hurt that I've locked myself away from the possibility of being happy. And Caleb's out there, waiting. Proving every single day that he meant what he said.

I sit up in bed, my heart pounding.

What am I doing?

The man I love is waiting for me. He's been waiting patiently. Giving me space while reminding me he's here by leaving flowers and succulents, sending casseroles and cheeseburgers, showing me in every way he can think of that he's not going anywhere. And I'm lying here, miserable, because I'm too scared to believe him.

Mom was wrong. She was wrong about Dad, and she was wrong about all the men after him, because she chose the wrong ones. She expected them to leave, so she never really let them in. And then when they did leave, it just confirmed what she already believed.

But Caleb isn't like them. He stayed. Caleb is still here.

It's time to stop running.

I throw off the covers before I can talk myself out of it.

Then I stop. It's Friday. I have twenty-two second graders expecting me in a few hours.

For a moment, I hesitate. I've never called in sick when there wasn't an emergency. But some things can't wait.

I pick up my phone and dial the school's substitute line. My voice only shakes a little when I leave the message. "This is Willow Dawson. I need to take a personal day today. I'm sorry for the short notice. Emergency sub plans are in the red folder on top of the bookshelf behind my desk."

I hang up before I can change my mind.

Outside, the sky is just starting to lighten. I pull on my boots and jacket and head to the barn. Clover nickers when she sees me, expecting her breakfast.

"Hey, girl." I let myself into her stall and wrap my arms around her neck. She stands patiently, letting me hold on the way she always does. "I'm going to do something scary today."

She bumps her nose against my shoulder.

"I'm going to tell him I was wrong. I'm going to ask him to give me another chance." My voice wavers. "What if he says no? What if I hurt him too badly?"

Clover snorts softly, and I swear she's telling me to stop being ridiculous.

"You're right." I pull back and look at her. "He's been showing me he still cares all week. He's not going to say no."

I feed her and make sure she has fresh water. Then I stand at the stall door for a moment longer.

"Wish me luck," I say.

She whinnies, and I choose to take that as encouragement.

Back in the house, I shower and stand in front of my closet, staring at my clothes like I've never seen them before. What do you wear to win back the man you love? Something pretty, but not like I'm trying too hard. Something that says I'm serious, but also sorry.

I choose a soft blue sweater that Caleb once said brought out my eyes and pull on my nicest jeans. I brush my hair until it shines and put on just a little makeup to hide the evidence of too many sleepless nights.

I catch my reflection in the mirror and barely recognize myself. Not because I look different, but because something in my eyes has changed.

The fear is still there, but it's quieter now. Underneath it, there's determination.

Hope.

I grab my keys and stop in the kitchen, staring at the roses on my table and the succulent on my windowsill.

I'll wait as long as it takes.

"You don't have to wait anymore," I whisper.

The drive to the ranch feels endless. My heart pounds the whole way, and I have to grip the steering wheel to keep my hands from trembling. What if he's changed his mind? What if I took too long? What if I've ruined everything and he doesn't want me anymore?

I pass the turnoff for town, then the old oak tree that marks the halfway point between my place and Apple Blossom Ranch. The fields stretch out on either side of the road, just starting to turn green with the first hints of spring.

Spring. New beginnings. Maybe that's what this is.

But then the seed of doubt creeps back in. I picture his face when I told him I couldn't do this anymore. The way his voice cracked when he said he'd wait. The hurt in his eyes that he tried so hard to hide.

I did that to him. I caused that pain.

What if he forgives me but can't forget? What if there's too much damage to repair?

I almost turn around twice. My hands shake so badly at one point that I have to pull over to the side of the road and just breathe.

But then I remember his words. The card. The roses. The succulent with its tiny tag.

Still here.

He's still here. He's been telling me since I left that he's still here.

I pull back onto the road and keep driving.

The entrance to Apple Blossom Ranch comes into view, and my stomach flips. I turn down the long driveway, passing the main house where Finn and Patty live. Smoke curls up from the chimney.

Caleb's cottage sits at the edge of the property, tucked back near the tree line. It's small but well-kept, with a porch that wraps around the front. I pull up just as the sun breaks over the horizon, painting the sky in shades of pink and gold. His truck is in the driveway.

He's home.

For a long moment, I just sit there, staring at the front door and trying to gather my courage. My heart is beating so hard I can feel it in my throat.

I can do this. I can be brave. I can choose love over fear.

I get out of the car before I can change my mind.

My legs feel unsteady as I walk up the porch steps. The boards creak under my feet, impossibly loud in the early morning quiet. I raise my hand to knock, but the door swings open before my knuckles touch the wood.

Caleb stands there in jeans and a flannel shirt, his hair messy like he just woke up. There are shadows under his eyes that weren't there before. He looks tired. Like he hasn't been sleeping any better than I have.

His eyes widen when he sees me. "Willow?"

"I was wrong." The words tumble out before I can stop them. "I was scared and I pushed you away and I'm so sorry. I know I hurt you. I know I don't deserve another chance. But I love you, Caleb. I love you so much, and I don't want to spend another day pretending I don't."

He doesn't say anything. He just stares at me, his expression unreadable.

My heart sinks. "If you've changed your mind, I understand. I wouldn't blame you. I just needed you to know that I—"

He moves so fast I don't have time to finish. One second he's standing in the doorway, the next his arms are around me, pulling me against his chest so tight I can barely breathe.

"I haven't changed my mind," he says into my hair. "I could never change my mind about you."

The tears come then, hot and fast, soaking into his shirt. "I'm sorry," I say again. "I'm so sorry."

"Shh." He pulls back just enough to cup my face in his hands, wiping my tears with his thumbs. His eyes are wet too, I realize. "You're here now. That's all that matters."

"I was so scared."

"I know."

"I thought if I ended it first, it wouldn't hurt as much when you left."

"I was never going to leave." He holds my gaze, steady and sure. "I told you, Willow. I'm not going anywhere."

"I believe you." And for the first time, I really do. The words seep into my bones, into my heart, into all the broken places I've been carrying around since I was ten years old. "I believe you."

He smiles, and it's like watching the sun come out after a week of rain. "Yeah?"

"Yeah." I laugh through my tears. "I'm sorry it took me so long to figure it out."

"I'd have waited longer." He brushes a strand of hair from my face, his touch so gentle it makes me want to cry all over again. "I'd have waited forever."

"You don't have to wait anymore."

"Good." He leans down and kisses me, soft and sweet and full of promise. I melt into him, my hands gripping the front of his shirt, holding on like I'll never let go. "Because I really missed you," he murmurs against my lips.

"I missed you too." I wrap my arms around his neck and hold on tight. "I missed you so much."

He pulls me closer, and I breathe him in. Coffee and cedar and something that's just him. The smell I've been missing all week.

"Do you have time to come inside?" he asks. "I'll make you breakfast."

"I took the day off work, but you don't have to—"

"I want to." He takes my hand and leads me through the door. "I've been eating cereal for a week because I couldn't be bothered to cook. You're giving me an excuse."

I laugh, and the sound surprises me. I didn't think I'd be laughing this morning. I thought I'd be terrified and anxious and possibly rejected. Instead, I'm standing in Caleb's kitchen while he makes a fresh pot of coffee, and everything feels right for the first time in days.

"Thank you," I say quietly.

He looks up from the coffeemaker. "For what?"

"For not giving up on me. For the roses. For the succulent. For the card. For the casseroles. And the burger and–." I swallow hard. "For loving me even when I was too scared to let you."

He crosses the kitchen and takes my face in his hands again. "Willow, I will always love you. Even when you're scared. Even when you push me away. That's not going to change."

"Promise?"

"Promise." He kisses my forehead. "Now sit down and let me make you pancakes."

TIA MARLEE

I sit at his small kitchen table and watch him move around the kitchen, cracking eggs and frying bacon. The sun streams through the window, warm and golden. Outside, I can hear birds singing.

This is real. This is happening. I chose love, and love chose me back.

Maybe I finally found my happy ending.

Chapter Seventeen

Caleb

Willow's sitting at my kitchen table, watching me make pancakes, and I keep having to remind myself this is real.

She's here. She came back. She chose me.

The morning light catches the gold in her hair as she wraps her hands around a cup of coffee. She looks tired, but there's a softness in her face that wasn't there when she showed up on my porch.

"These might be terrible," I warn her, flipping a pancake. "I'm not much of a cook."

"I don't care." She smiles, and my heart stutters. "I'm just happy to be here."

I slide a plate in front of her and sit down across the table. For a moment, we just look at each other. There's so much I want to say, so much I want to ask, but I don't want to push. She's here. That's enough for now.

"Eat," I say. "Before they get cold."

She takes a bite and her eyebrows rise. "These are actually good."

"Thank goodness."

She laughs, and the sound fills all the empty spaces that have been aching for a week. I could listen to that laugh for the rest of my life.

My phone buzzes on the counter. I glance at it and see Austin's name.

"Work?" Willow asks.

"Probably wondering where I am." I pick up the phone and type a quick message. *Taking a personal day. On call if there's an emergency.*

His response comes immediately. *About time. Tell Willow I said hi.*

I shake my head. Small towns.

"Everything okay?" Willow asks.

"Perfect." I set the phone down and reach across the table for her hand. "I told Austin I'm taking the day off. I want to spend it with you."

Her fingers lace through mine. "You don't have to do that."

"I want to." I rub my thumb across her knuckles. "There's something I want to show you. If you're up for it."

"What is it?"

"It's a surprise." I grin at her curious expression. "Finish your pancakes first."

We clean up the kitchen together, moving around each other with an easy rhythm that feels natural. Like we've been doing this for years. A taste of what could be for the rest of our lives.

I grab a blanket from the closet and lead her outside. The morning is cool but clear, the sky a brilliant blue. Spring is definitely coming. The trees are budding, and somewhere in the distance I can hear birds singing.

"Where are we going?" Willow asks as I lead her across the property.

"You'll see."

We walk past the main barn, the paddocks where Finn keeps his horses, and the apple orchard that gave the ranch its name. Willow's hand stays in mine the whole way, her fingers warm and her grip steady.

Finally, we reach the east pasture. The land slopes gently down toward a creek that runs along the edge of the property. Wildflowers are just starting to push through the grass, dots of purple and yellow against the green.

"Caleb." Willow's voice is soft. "This is beautiful."

"It's my favorite spot on the whole ranch." I spread the blanket on the grass and sit down, pulling her down beside me. "I used to come here when I was a kid, when we'd visit Uncle Harry. I'd sit right here and watch the horses graze and dream about the future."

She leans into my side, and I wrap my arm around her. "What did you dream about?"

"Different things, depending on the year. Being a cowboy. Being a vet. Having my own place someday." I pause, looking out over the pasture. "Lately, I've been dreaming about something else."

"What?"

I take a breath. This is the moment.

"I talked to Finn a few weeks ago. Before everything happened." I turn to look at her. "I asked him if I could build a house here. On this spot."

Her eyes widen. "You did?"

"I've been picturing it in my head. A house with a big porch, right here, facing the pasture. A kitchen with lots of counter space, because you deserve better than that cramped one you have now." I smile. "A primary bedroom with windows facing east, so the morning sun wakes us up."

Willow's quiet, her eyes glistening.

"And over there," I continue, pointing toward a flat stretch of land near the creek, "I pictured a barn. A nice one, with plenty of stalls. One for Clover, obviously. And room for whatever other horses we might want someday."

"Caleb..." Her voice breaks.

"I pictured you waking up every morning and looking out the window and seeing your horses grazing right outside. I pictured us drinking coffee on the porch and watching the sunset. I pictured..." I swallow hard. "I pictured a life. *Our* lives. Together."

She turns to face me, tears streaming down her cheeks. "You thought about all of that?"

"I've thought about it every day since the night I met you." I reach up and wipe her tears with my thumb. "I know it's a lot. I know we haven't been together that long. And I know you're still healing from everything that happened with your dad and your mom and all the years of being afraid."

She nods, her lower lip trembling.

"So I'm not asking you to decide anything right now." I take her hands in mine. "I'm just telling you what I see when I imagine my future. And you're in every single part of it."

"Caleb." She squeezes my hands so tight it almost hurts. "I don't know what to say."

"You don't have to say anything. I just wanted you to know." I lean my forehead against hers. "When you're ready, Willow. Whenever that is. I'll be here. We can build this together, at whatever pace feels right to you."

She's quiet for a long moment, and I hold my breath. Then she pulls back and looks at me with those beautiful dark eyes, still wet with tears but shining with hope.

"I want that," she whispers. "I want all of it. The house, the barn, the horses. Waking up next to you every morning." She laughs, a little shakily.

I laugh too, the sound catching in my throat. "Yeah?"

"Yeah." She cups my face in her hands. "I don't know when I'll be ready for all the official stuff. The ring and the wedding and everything. But I know I want a future with you, Caleb. I'm not scared of that anymore."

I kiss her then, slow and deep, pouring everything I feel into it. The love, the relief, the overwhelming gratitude that she came back to me. That she chose us.

When we break apart, she's smiling a smile that reaches her eyes and lights up her whole face.

"I love you," I say.

"I love you, too."

We lie back on the blanket and stare up at the sky. Her head is on my chest and my arm is around her shoulders. The sun is warm, the grass is soft, and somewhere in the distance, the creek bubbles over the rocks like quiet laughter drifting through the breeze.

"Clover's going to love it here," Willow says.

"I know." I press a kiss to the top of her head. "That's why I picked this spot."

She tilts her head up to look at me. "You picked this spot for Clover?"

"I picked this spot for you. But I knew you'd never be happy without Clover nearby." I smile. "I figured if I was going to convince you to spend your life with me, I'd better make sure there was room for your horse."

She laughs again, a beautiful sound that I want to hear every day for the rest of my life. "You really do know me."

"I'm trying to." I tighten my arm around her. "I want to spend the rest of my life learning everything there is to know about you, Willow Dawson."

She snuggles closer, and we watch the clouds drift overhead. I think about everything that led us here. The emergency call. The scared woman in the barn. The walls she built and the patience it took to earn her trust.

It wasn't easy. But nothing worth having ever is.

"Hey, Caleb?" Willow says after a while.

"Yeah?"

"Thank you for not giving up on me."

I kiss her forehead. "Never. Not in a million years."

We stay there until the sun is high in the sky, talking about everything and nothing. Making plans. Dreaming out loud. For the first time in my life, the future feels real and solid and full of possibility.

I'm going to marry this woman someday. I'm going to build her a house with a big porch and a barn for her horses. I'm going to wake up next to her every morning and thank God she chose me.

But for now, this is enough. Her in my arms. The sun on our faces. The promise of everything still to come.

For now, this is everything.

Chapter Eighteen

Willow

Three months later

I barely recognize myself. Not on the outside. I still look the same, I still wear my hair the same way, I still show up to school every morning with lesson plans and a travel mug of coffee. But something inside me has shifted. The fear that used to live in my chest, that constant low hum of waiting for everything to fall apart, has quieted.

It's not completely gone. I don't know if it ever will be. But it's manageable now. Background noise instead of a siren.

"You're glowing," Becca says, sliding into the seat across from me in the teacher's lounge. "It's disgusting."

I laugh. "I am not glowing."

"You positively are. You've been glowing for months. The kids have noticed. Mrs. Patterson asked me if you'd changed your skincare routine." She steals a carrot from my lunch. "I told her it's not skincare, it's regular access to a swoony veterinarian."

"Becca!"

"What? It's true." She grins. "So how are things? Still perfect?"

"Things are good." I can't help the smile that spreads across my face. "Really good."

"Just good?" She raises an eyebrow. "Last week you told me he brought you flowers for no reason. The week before that, he surprised you with a picnic. And didn't he just help you fix that fence at your place?"

"He did." The memory of Caleb sweating in the spring sunshine, working alongside me to repair the paddock fence, makes butterflies take flight in my stomach. "He's wonderful, Becca. I don't know how else to say it."

"You could say you're madly in love and planning to spend the rest of your life with him."

I look down at my sandwich. "We've talked about it. The future, I mean. He showed me this spot on the ranch where he wants to build a house someday. With a barn for Clover."

Becca's eyes go wide. "Willow. That's huge."

"I know."

"That's marriage-level planning."

"I know." I can't stop smiling. "He said when I'm ready. No pressure. Whenever I'm ready, he'll be there."

"And?" She leans forward. "Are you ready?"

I think about it. I've been thinking about it for weeks now. The fear that used to scream at me to run, to protect myself, to keep my walls up is barely a whisper now.

"I think I might be," I admit. "Or getting there, at least."

Becca reaches across the table and squeezes my hand. "I'm so happy for you. You deserve this."

"Thanks." My throat tightens. "I wasn't sure I'd ever get here, you know? After everything with my mom, and growing up the way I did... I thought I was broken. I thought I'd never be able to trust anyone enough to let them in."

"But you did."

"But I did." I squeeze her hand back. "He made it easy. He just kept showing up, kept proving that he meant what he said. Eventually, I ran out of reasons not to believe him."

"How are things with your mom?" Becca asks carefully. "After everything that happened when she visited?"

I consider the question. "We talk sometimes. Not often, but more than before. I think her visit was actually a turning point for me. Just not the way she intended."

"What do you mean?"

"She showed me what I didn't want to become." I say it gently, without bitterness. "Fifty-two and still convinced that love always ends in heartbreak. Still running from one relationship to the next, never letting anyone really in." I shake my head. "I don't want that. I refuse to let fear decide my future. Her story doesn't have to be my story."

Becca smiles. "Look at you, all wise and self-aware."

"Don't get used to it. I'm sure I'll spiral about something next week."

She laughs. "That's the Willow I know."

The bell rings, signaling the end of lunch. Becca stands and gathers her things.

"You two are coming to the spring festival next weekend, right?" she asks.

"We'll be there. Caleb's already planning which food trucks to hit."

She laughs. "Of course he is. See you later, lovebird."

I watch her go, still smiling. *Lovebird.* A few months ago, that word would have made me flinch. Now it just makes me happy.

After school, I drive home to feed Clover and change before my date with Caleb. It's become our Friday routine. Dinner at Beats and Eats, then maybe a movie at his cottage or a walk around the ranch if the weather's nice.

I used to be afraid of relationships like this. They felt like traps, like ways to get too comfortable before everything fell apart. Now I understand that routines aren't traps when you care about someone. They're foundations. They're the small, steady bricks that build a life.

Clover nickers when I walk into the barn, already expecting her evening grain.

"Hey, girl." I rub her nose and she pushes into my hand. "Guess what? You might be getting a new barn soon. A really nice one, with a view of the creek."

She snorts, unimpressed.

"I know, I know. You're perfectly happy here." I give her one more pat before heading to the feed room. "But just wait until you see the pasture. You're going to love it."

I finish my barn chores and head inside to shower and change. I catch myself putting in a little extra effort tonight, choosing the blue sweater Caleb likes and actually doing something with my hair. Not because I need to impress him. Just because I want to. Because making an effort for someone you love isn't a burden. It's a joy.

When I pull up to Beats and Eats, Caleb's truck is already in the parking lot. He's leaning against it, waiting for me, and my heart skips when I see him. He offered to pick me up, but I told him I'd meet him, instead.

"Hey, beautiful." He pulls me into a hug and kisses the top of my head. "How was your day?"

"Good. Long. Better now."

He takes my hand and leads me inside. The dinner rush hasn't started yet, so the restaurant is quiet. Ms. Daisy is behind the counter, wiping down menus, and her face lights up when she sees us.

"Well, well, well." She sets down her rag and plants her hands on her hips. "My two favorite customers. Together again. What a surprise."

"Hi, Ms. Daisy," I say, sliding into our usual booth.

"Don't you 'hi Ms. Daisy' me." She follows us to the table, pulling out her notepad. "You two have been coming in here every Friday for months now. Same booth, same googly eyes at each other, same disgustingly adorable hand-holding."

Caleb grins. "Is that a problem?"

"The only problem is you haven't put a ring on this girl's finger yet." She points her pen at him. "What are you waiting for, Caleb Miller? An engraved invitation?"

I feel my cheeks flush. "Ms. Daisy—"

"Don't you start. I've known this boy since he was running around in diapers, and I've never seen him look at anyone the way he looks at you." She turns back to Caleb. "So? When are you going to make it official?"

Caleb glances at me, his eyes warm. "When she's ready."

Ms. Daisy looks between us, and her expression softens. "Well, that's the right answer, I suppose." She tucks her notepad into her apron. "But don't wait too long. Life's short, and love like this doesn't come around every day."

She bustles off to get our drinks, and I turn to Caleb with a laugh.

"She's not subtle, is she?"

"Never has been." He reaches across the table and takes my hand. "She's right, though. About one thing, at least."

"What's that?"

"Love like this doesn't come around every day." He rubs his thumb across my knuckles. "I got lucky, Willow."

"We both did."

Jolene appears with our drinks and takes our order. Same thing we always get. Caleb's cheeseburger with extra pickles, my bacon cheeseburger with sweet potato fries.

"I talked to Becca today," I say after Jolene leaves. "About us. The future."

"Yeah?" Caleb's eyes search my face. "What did you tell her?"

"I told her you showed me the spot where you want to build a house. That you said you'd wait until I was ready." I take a breath. "And I told her I think I might be getting there."

His hand tightens on mine. "Willow..."

"I'm not saying we need to rush anything. I'm just saying..." I meet his eyes. "I'm not scared anymore. Not of you, not of us, not of the future. For the first time in my life, I'm excited about what comes next instead of dreading it."

Caleb is quiet for a moment. Then he lifts my hand to his lips and kisses my knuckles.

"That's all I ever wanted," he says softly. "For you to feel safe enough to be excited about the future."

"I do. Because of you."

"Because of us."

I smile. "Because of us."

Ms. Daisy returns with our food, and we eat and talk and laugh like we always do. The restaurant fills up around us, but I barely notice. My whole world has narrowed to the man sitting across from me, to the life we're building together.

After we finish eating, Caleb pays the bill and waves goodbye to Ms. Daisy. She winks at him and mouths "ring" while pointing at me, and I have to cover my mouth to keep from laughing.

Outside, the sun is setting, painting the sky in vibrant shades of orange and pink. Caleb pulls me close, and we stand there in the parking lot, watching the colors fade.

"I love you," he says.

"I love you, too."

It's simple. It's routine. It's everything I never knew I needed.

And for the first time in my life, I'm not waiting for the other shoe to drop. I'm not bracing for impact. I'm just here, in this moment, with this man, trusting that tomorrow will be just as good as today.

Maybe even better.

That's what love is. Not the absence of fear, but the presence of something stronger. Something worth fighting for.

Something worth believing in.

I finally found it. And I'm never letting go.

Epilogue – 5 Months Later

Cooper

The Oklahoma sun beats down on my back as I finish shoeing the last horse of the day. She's a beautiful mare, high-strung and expensive, owned by an older woman who treats her horses better than most people treat their kids.

"Perfect as always, Cooper." Mrs. Whitman hands me a check and a bottle of water. "Same time next month?"

"Yes, ma'am." I tuck the check into my pocket, tip my hat, and load my tools into the back of my truck.

This is my life. Has been for the past few years. I travel the show circuit, moving from barn to barn, state to state, shoeing horses for people with more money than sense. It's good work. Steady. Pays well.

But lately, it's started to feel empty.

I lean against my truck and drink the water, watching the activity around the show grounds. Trainers schooling horses. Grooms rushing around with buckets and brushes. Riders in pristine outfits practicing their form.

None of it feels like home.

Home is Apple Blossom Ranch. Home is the smell of apple blossoms in spring and the sound of the creek running past the east pasture. Home is Sunday dinners, Caleb's terrible jokes, and the feeling of belonging somewhere.

I've been running from home for years. Told myself I needed space, needed freedom, needed to make my own way. And I did. I built a successful business. I've got clients all over the Midwest who request me by name.

But what's the point of success if you've got no one to share it with?

My phone buzzes in my pocket. I pull it out and see Caleb's name on the screen.

"Hey, big brother," I answer. "What's up?"

"You busy?"

"Just finished a job. Why?"

There's a pause on the other end. When Caleb speaks again, I can hear the smile in his voice. "I'm going to ask Willow to marry me."

I straighten up, a grin spreading across my face. "About time. When?"

"Two weeks from Saturday. I want to do it at the ranch, at the spot where I'm going to build our house." He pauses. "I want everyone there, Coop. You, Colton, Holly. Uncle Harry and Aunt Maggie are flying in from Florida. Finn's already in on it. He's helping me plan."

"You want me to come home?"

"I want you to be there when I ask the woman I love to spend the rest of her life with me." His voice softens. "You're my brother. I need you there."

An ache starts in my chest. I should be there. Home. With my family. Things are changing so fast, and I'm missing it.

"I'll be there," I say, already thinking of who I can give my work to.

"Yeah?"

"Yeah. Wouldn't miss it."

We talk for a few more minutes. He tells me about the plan, about how he's going to involve Clover somehow, about the ring he picked out with Patty's help. He sounds happier than I've ever heard him. Content in a way I didn't know was possible.

After we hang up, I stand there for a long time, staring at nothing.

Caleb found his person. Finn found his. Even Uncle Harry found love after all those years alone.

What am I doing out here?

I think about the conversation I had with Finn a few months back. He mentioned they could use a full-time farrier at the ranch. Said there was room for me if I ever wanted to come back.

At the time, I brushed it off. I wasn't ready. Too restless, too stubborn, too determined to prove I could make it on my own.

But maybe being on your own isn't all it's cracked up to be.

I climb into my truck and sit behind the wheel, thinking.

Two weeks. That's how long I have before Caleb's proposal. Plenty of time to finish up my current clients, tie up loose ends, and figure out what comes next.

Or maybe I already know what comes next.

I pull out my phone and dial Finn's number.

"Cooper?" He sounds surprised. "Everything okay?"

"Yeah. Everything's good." I take a breath. "That offer you made a few months ago. About coming home. Working at the ranch."

There's a pause. "What about it?"

"Is it still on the table?"

Another pause, longer this time. When Finn speaks again, I can hear the smile in his voice. "It never left the table, Coop. You know that."

"Good." I start the engine. "Because I think it's time I came home."

"For Caleb's thing? Or for good?"

I look out the windshield at the Oklahoma landscape. Rolling hills, endless sky, nothing that feels like mine.

"Both," I say. "I'm ready to put down some roots."

Finn laughs, warm and genuine. "About time, little brother. About time."

Thank you so much for reading His to Hold. Caleb and Willow stole my heart. I love a man who is strong and steady for the woman he loves. If you enjoyed this story, I would appreciate it if you'd consider leaving a review. Even a star rating helps other readers know if it might be a book they would like.

Want to read all about their proposal? Grab your FREE bonus content when you join my newsletter.

His to Love is coming soon! Make sure you've joined my newsletter list, or follow me on social media so you don't miss any updates! In the meantime, check out my Sugar & Sirens series also in Kindle Unlimited!

About Tia

Tia Marlee resides in Central Texas with her husband and three teenage children. When she isn't writing, Tia enjoys reading, embroidery and spending time with her family. Tia is the author of sweet, no-steam, small-town, contemporary romance and romantic comedy. Her books are like Hallmark meets real life with a dash of humor.

Follow Tia on Facebook, Instagram, or check out her website for more information.

Also By Tia Marlee

Piney Brook Wishes Series

His Christmas Wish

Sweet Summertime Wishes

Wishing for the Girl Next Door

A Soldier's Wish

Her New Year's Wish

The Piney Brook Wishes Box Set

The Coffee Loft Series

Bean Wishing for a Latte Love

You Mocha Me Crazy

A Brewtiful Kind of Love

Coffee Loft Collection

Apple Blossom Ranch Series

His to Adore
His to Have
His to Hold
His to Love
His to Cherish
Hers to Treasure

Sugar and Sirens
Still Yours, Always Mine
Catch Me, If You Can
Sweeter With You
A Little Bit Married
The Last First Kiss

A Little Bit of Christmas
Merry & Bright: The Great Light Fight
Gnome Sweet Home
The Candy Cane Parade
Mistletoe at Midnight

Let's Stay In Touch

You can find me at my website: https://tiamarlee.com
Follow me:
Facebook: https://tinyurl.com/FBTiaMarlee
Instagram: https://tinyurl.com/IGTiaMarlee
Amazon: https://tinyurl.com/AmazonTiaMarlee
BookBub: https://tinyurl.com/BBTiaMarlee
Goodreads: https://tinyurl.com/GRTiaMarlee

Join my reader group: https://tinyurl.com/TiaMarleeReaderGroup

www.ingramcontent.com/pod-product-compliance
Lightning Source LLC
Chambersburg PA
CBHW022024170626
46808CB00003B/1052